SAMMI AND THE JERSEY BULL

FURRY UNITED COALITION NEWBIE ACADEMY

C.D. GORRI

Produced in Canada

An EveL Worlds Production : www.worlds.EveLanglais.com

Edited by BookNookNuts

ACKNOWLEDGMENTS

Here I go again! I can't tell you how super-blessed I feel to write in EveL Worlds! THANK YOU Eve Langlais for letting me play in your sandbox!

Xoxo, C.D.

P.S. A special thank you to the amazing Jess Ripley for letting me pick your beautiful brain about Canadian legal documents and your input on the Queen scam. You rock! xoxo

AUTHOR'S NOTE

Hello Awesome Readers!

Thank you for grabbing this FUC Academy story. I am such a huge fan of this world created by the incomparable Eve Langlais and am truly honored to take part in this venture. I hope you enjoy reading about a Jersey Bull with questionable familial affiliations and a prickly hedgie who sure as heck turns out to be his mate!

I look forward to adding more to the series soon!

Happy reading!
Xoxo,
C.D. Gorri

PROLOGUE

"I was just wondering why we still use the image of a scarab to represent SCAR, sir" Harrison Greymole looked down nervously as he addressed his master. "I mean the detectives now associate us with the beetle."

"Beetle? Did you say beetle? The scarab is sacred, Harrison," Dr. Wembley Ranklinger the sixth growled at him between clenched teeth as he worked.

The leader of *Shifter Capture Alteration and Removal*, or SCAR, came from a long line of doctors dedicated to protecting humanity by destroying the terrible shifter infestation that was endangering the world.

After months of experimentation and rehabilitation, Harrison finally understood just how lucky he was to have been chosen by the man standing next to him. And to think, he had been cured with no pain or permanent malformation, unlike some of the good doctor's experiments.

Well, mostly. There was the unfortunate crisscrossed scarring on his face, neck, and stomach. But those could all be corrected with plastic surgery. He was sure of it. His master would not leave him to remain permanently on the outskirts of society because of the necessary procedures used to cure him.

Dr. Ranklinger was a genius and a kind man motivated by his desire to keep the world safe for humankind. Harrison did so want to aid him.

He watched his master, currently bent at the waist, butt in the air, and head cocked to the side, as he continued to work. An odd angle for sure, but it in no way decimated Harrison's respect and affection for the man. Even if Dr. Ranklinger did recently cut the star tip right off the former mole shifter's nose, leaving a gaping hole in his face that was difficult to look at.

He made us better. He made us human, and to be human is to be perfect.

Shhh. He scolded that part of him that still tried to communicate every now and again.

Had to keep that under wraps. The doctor would put him back in the experimentation process, and Harrison had enough treatment. He was perfect now.

Yes, he was sure of it.

"We use the scarab because, Harrison," grunted the good doctor, "it is tradition."

"Of course, sir." Harrison nodded.

He watched as Ranklinger slid a pair of protective goggles over his eyes, making his soulless black peepers appear ten times the size they normally were. Then his master used a precision laser pen to cut the image of the scarab used to represent SCAR into the cornerstone of the warehouse where they'd performed their latest experiments.

"Did you call the hotline yet, Harrison?"

"I called in the tip earlier today. By the time those PRICs

decipher it, we will be long gone. But have you finished with the female already, master?"

"I have. My goal with her is different from the others." Ranklinger chuckled, and Harrison nodded with glee.

Oh, the honor! As a lowly mole shifter, Harrison had never been included in activities the other supernaturals in his hometown had taken part in. He was often overlooked. Lonely and alone, that was how he'd lived.

Until Dr. Ranklinger. He alone saw Harrison's value. Calling Harrison into his service and showing him his true purpose! To aid the secret organization that worked toward the complete abolishment of shifters!

Yes. Harrison Greymole was *hashtag blessed*, as the normals often said on their little social media platforms.

Such clever creatures recording every instance of their lives to share with the entire world. Shifters did not have that freedom. How pathetic for them to have to hide. Dr. Ranklinger was right. They would be better off gone. Wiped clean from history.

"I will show that PRIC what it means to mess with me." Dr. Ranklinger gritted his yellowed teeth.

"Excellent, sir!" Harrison applauded his master's plan.

Still, he wondered if the genius doctor should have maybe set the timer for the minor explosion to go off a little later in the night. As it was, they were cutting it close.

The crash and boom of the small dirty bomb that Harrison had built suddenly went off in the tiny office he'd cleaned out earlier that day.

Well, he'd mostly cleaned it out. After all, the explosion would take care of the rest of the mess he'd left behind. He was sure of it.

There was just so much to do in one day! It was difficult being a human minion.

The force of the blast sent Dr. Ranklinger and Harrison flying backward onto the dirty, broken asphalt of the parking lot behind the abandoned warehouse.

"Dammit, Harrison. I said set the timer for eight minutes to ten!"

"Oh," Harrison squeaked, a remnant of his former shifter days before Dr. Ranklinger had found and cured him. "I thought you said ten to eight. My humble apologies, master-"

"Don't call me *master*! I am a doctor, Harrison. Dr. Ranklinger!"

Yes. He was a doctor. An educated man. Unlike Harrison Greymole, the poor janitor who worked in the building where Ranklinger's old condominium was located.

Harrison didn't recall seeing a diploma from any medical school anywhere in Dr. Ranklinger's *Place of Operations*. That was *POO* for short.

Well, *er*, at any rate, Harrison was trying out the nickname. Having invented it himself, he was proud of the rather clever acronym.

"Let's go, Harrison"—Ranklinger snapped his fingers at his minion—"before someone comes."

"Yes, sir. Right away, sir." Harrison scurried. "Let's hurry back home to *POO*!"

Dr. Ranklinger slapped himself on the forehead. Uh-oh. Harrison knew that did not bode well for his immediate future.

Sigh. He was sure to get dog food for supper again. But he'd had worse. At least he was sure he must have. Why else would he be there? He turned his head to the good doctor, who was snapping again, directly in Harrison's face.

"How many times do I have to tell you not to call it that?"

Ranklinger shouted as they hurried away to where they'd left the car.

Dust and debris scattered with the wind across the lot and sidewalk. The sting of black smoke billowing out from the warehouse made his lungs burn and his eyes tear.

Master was right. He was *always* right. Another explosion sounded.

Squeak!

"Hurry, you useless rodent!" Ranklinger snarled, "We need to leave before that PRIC arrives!"

"Yes, maste-, I mean, yes, Doctor." Harrison scurried behind him. He wondered why his master always called him a rodent, when he was clearly an insectivore.

He only hoped the little mouse would be okay. Harrison was useless, as the doctor said, but he was not a murderer.

He bit his fingernails and silently wished for the PRICs to come fast.

1

A few hours later...

Agents and firefighters scrambled to control the blaze currently burning its way through an empty section of warehouses in one of the worst parts of the neighborhood.

It was a good thing the shifter organization known as Private Resourceful Investigative Contractors, known as PRIC for short, intercepted the call before the locals could seize command.

Humans tended to muck things up when supes were involved. Sergio sucked in a breath of clean fresh air upon emerging from one of the burning buildings. He looked down at the bundle in his arms and frowned.

The female was unconscious from smoke inhalation but otherwise seemed unharmed. He had no doubt from the pictures her brother, fellow PRIC Detective Tony Leeds, had sent every member of their agency that this was, in fact, the missing mouse shifter, Julietta DiCarlo.

She was one of seven siblings from Leeds' adoptive family. The Jersey Devil shifter had been taken in by them when he was just a child. That meant the little mouse shifter was family to every PRIC involved in her rescue as well. Including Sergio.

The firefighters on the scene had assured him the warehouse was empty, but after years of hunting lost shifters, Sergio had developed a sixth sense for these things. That and the tip he'd received earlier that day led him to check the rooms deep underground while the brave men and women of the 118, a shifter-run fire station, battled the flames above.

He'd gotten lucky. Saved the girl before the fire could eat its way through to her cell. The animals who'd kidnapped her had left her to burn!

Bastards. His bull snorted angrily, but Sergio held a leash on his inner beast. Refusing to give way to the rage that built inside him.

A special helicopter had arrived to take the female to the Head Office for Life-threatening Emergencies to assess for internal damages. *HOLE* was packed with PRICs, ASSs, and FUCs by the time Sergio arrived with the female.

The pop-up clinics were used by joint task forces in the shifter world to make it easier to receive treatment for any injuries sustained on the job. Fast, easy, safe.

The pop-up clinics were the brainchild of Dr. Damon Finn, a python shifter and all-around unusual fellow. Sergio had no beef with him. In fact, he respected the man.

This was one such joint task force. Assigned to putting an end to the mysterious anti-shifter organization bent on experimentation to end all shifter-kind, nicknamed SCARAB by Tony Leeds himself. The Jersey Devil was renowned for his dedication and commitment to finding the evil group of demented psychopaths who hunted and experimented on shifters.

Everyone on the team was furious at the gang's unmitigated gall in kidnapping a family member of one of their own. PRIC detectives across the country had been updated on the progress, as had the other agencies as well. It was outrageous. And Sergio Gravino would not stand for it. He was going to find the bastards responsible for the heinous act.

He'd stayed by the victim's side until Dr. Finn's sedative took hold. She'd been sleeping soundly by the time he was ready to go, leaving her in the more-than-capable hands of the agents at HOLE.

Damon Finn was a devoted doctor and scientist. Not someone the bull shifter ran into on the regular, but he had a pristine reputation. Finn was an egghead, if you will, while Sergio's own tastes ran more toward the physically aggressive.

What else could he say? *Dammit, Finn. I'm a bull, not a doctor. Snort.* And that's what he got for staying up watching reruns the other night.

Once a Trekkie. Sigh. Good times.

At any rate, it was a good thing the SCARAB task force had their own HOLE. The clinic proved especially useful since this particular group of depraved individuals was infamous for causing head injuries. The kind that left permanent damage.

Unconscionable. Sergio aligned his sentiments with his fellow PRICs and the other agents in their anger and disgust. People like that did not deserve the humane treatment his organization, and the others, had always strived to offer their enemies.

Should go back to the old ways. Could always use fertilizer back on the farm.

His inner bull snorted in agreement. The animal was

bloodthirsty, for a vegetarian. The very thought of offering their foes any semblance of asylum was distasteful to his beast.

His bull's idea of *humane treatment* went along the lines of gouging their foes' hearts out with one of his mighty horns and leaving them to exsanguinate on the ground. But only after he'd trampled them with his sharp hooves, ensuring they felt every single one of his two-thousand pounds.

Good idea.

Grrr.

His bull was prone to rage. It was why he started taking meditative breathing classes online. Of course, they did not always help. Sometimes hard lessons needed to be learned.

Like now.

Sigh.

Breathe in. Breathe out.

Crap. Those breathing lessons were so not helping right now. He wanted to hunt down the bastards responsible for Julietta's kidnapping and attempted murder by arson. They deserved the harshest punishment, in his humble opinion.

"You all right?" Dr. Finn asked as he approached one of the several monitors connected to his patient.

Sergio nodded. But it was a lie. Truth was he hadn't felt right in weeks. Must be the heat. Summer in New Jersey could match any tropical climate, and he was due for a vacation. Not that he would take one until after this case was solved.

Grandpa Sal used to tease Sergio as a young bull. He'd say the phrase *bullheaded* came about for a reason. Then he'd claim Sergio was the reason.

There was some truth in it. Once Sergio had something in his head, he had a hell of a time letting it go. And he was not about to walk away from this case. The little mouse in the hospital bed squeaked as she sat up and peeked around the room, jarring him from his reverie.

"I can't believe all these people are here for me," Julietta squeaked from inside her hospital bed, and every protective instinct he had went haywire.

"Believe it, kiddo," he replied with a kind smile. "You feeling better?"

"Oh yes," she sighed. "Better now that I know you're here."

Uh-oh. The tiny female was staring at him with wide eyes. A little misplaced hero worship, he was sure. It sort of went with the territory. He shook his head and broke eye contact. Misleading the victim he'd saved? That was not part of his job.

2

Life had been hectic as all get-out from the moment Julietta's car had been discovered with the spoiled remnants of her grocery shopping one day after her abduction.

She was so small. Sergio could hardly believe she was full grown. In truth, she looked no more than thirteen or fourteen years old. A cute kid, but still too young for him, even though he knew she had to be old enough to drive.

Dr. Finn was scowling as he took in the exchange. He turned around and grabbed her chart quickly. The action more telling than he'd have liked. Sergio was sure of that.

Still, his bull did not care for the doctor's curt manner, and he growled at the python shifter. The man continued to work, unaffected. But he did not know why the doc should be so grumpy. Fucker needed to work on his bedside manner.

"Thank you, Sergio." The little mouse smiled up at him and batted her eyes.

"Uh, no problem, kid," he said, patting her hand before he left.

He knew she'd been checked for serious injury, and

other than a massive lump on the back of her noggin, she was okay.

"You know she thinks you're her personal hero, right?" Dr. Finn said without bothering to look up from his charts.

"What? No," Sergio grunted uncomfortably. "She's just a kid."

"She's twenty-six."

"Really? Shit. Well, doesn't matter to me. She's the sister of a colleague, and the victim of a terrible attack. My job is to find the assholes who did this. Nothing else," he informed the physician, who seemed to deflate once he gathered Sergio was telling the truth.

"Good," Dr. Finn said then walked away, leaving Sergio to contemplate the odd encounter.

He was profoundly grateful for the doctor's attentiveness to the victim. That Sergio had discovered the female safe and relatively unharmed gave him the satisfaction of a job well done. But that was as far as it went for him. Miss DiCarlo was no longer his business.

Whether it was pure luck or some integral part of a grander scheme he could not yet see, Sergio was glad he'd been on rotation when the anonymous tip that led him to the abandoned warehouse had come in over the wire.

Without it, he might never have found the young shifter. And saving shifters was what he did. Especially those girls who'd been ripped from the safety of their lives and locked away in a hellhole like that.

Sergio's mind kept racing over what he knew about the DiCarlo missing case file. Technically, he wasn't assigned to the growing task force dedicated to shutting down SCARAB.

Nope. He'd been on another case. Hot on the trail of an organization that seemed to profit from stolen identities. A bunch of veritable angels...*not.*

There were plenty of those types of miscreants going around, but these jokers had a predilection for stealing *shifter* identities. A little habit that got them noticed by PRICs, ASSs, and FUCs the world over.

It seemed they were getting more brazen in their crimes. Not only were victims' identities being stolen, and credits ruined, but people, *shifters*, were disappearing.

Normally a warehouse fire, even a suspicious one, was not Sergio's gig. But he was the next detective in line, or so Joe Canary, the boss' secretary, had informed him when the call came in.

Before that he'd been working the Spirito identity theft case. One of their frequent clients, Mrs. Bernadine Spirito lived down the shore by Maccon City, one of Sergio's favorite beach towns. She hired them to track down the person who'd been using her ten-year-old granddaughter's social security number to open up a slew of credit cards and bank loans.

The villain had racked up tens of thousands of dollars in debt so far. But every good PRIC knew that was only the beginning. After weeks of searching for the thief, Sergio had plenty of information but no real leads.

He'd compiled a list of cases similar to the Spirito girl's case and found several of them. All were still unsolved. There was one glaring difference, however. The young Spirito girl was about half the age of every other victim. The others were all college-aged shifters from various species all across the USA.

The most recent reports were from Pennsylvania, Oklahoma, Montana, California, and last, a young female college student, formerly from New Jersey, who'd gone missing over a year ago.

The woman, a *Samantha Andrews*, had told neighbors

she and her grandmother were moving to Canada, where she'd applied to the Furry United Coalition Newbie Academy, but neither had been seen or heard from again. Months had passed since the first report of her absence, and things were looking grim for the females.

Then, an anonymous tipster had called the *Private Resourceful Investigative Contractors Hotline*, or *1-87-PRIC-TIPS*, with the very information they needed leading to young Julietta's discovery and rescue.

A win for sure. Just not his win. Not that he wasn't more than thrilled to be part of the rescue. Still, something was bugging him. There was a part of this he just wasn't seeing clearly.

How did the two cases, the kidnapping and the identity thefts, tie together? Why was he given the tip that day from the hotline?

What if SCARAB was responsible for both?

The idea held merit. But he needed proof before presenting it to his boss.

Snort.

Poor little mouse had been handcuffed to a cot in what was little more than a holding pen. The old warehouse had been used to house animals for transport between zoos and circuses. But it had been closed down for years.

The stink of its former inhabitants was buried in the walls. Hard to get that out of your nostrils when you had super-sensitive noses.

But Julietta was safe now. Thank FUC for that, he thought. *Literally.*

It was a genuine team effort. He only hoped for similar happy endings for his other cases. After checking in on the female one last time, he left her resting peacefully back at HOLE.

Sergio headed back to the office to fill out all the necessary paperwork *in triplicate.*

Snort.

Margot Leeds—Tony's biological grandmother and the head of PRIC—did not trust computers. She insisted all the forms be filled out both online and by hand and filed accordingly.

Since it was a task force, he also had to copy every agency on his discoveries and his entire case.

Fucking hell.

He grabbed a large soft drink from the nearest drive-thru before settling in with a five-pound bag of baby carrots.

It was going to be a long night.

3

Furry United Coalition Newbie Academy, Canada

Six months earlier…

Samantha Marie Andrews barely held her anxiety in check. This was it. Her own personal D-day.

Sniff. Huff. Gasp.

Uh-oh.

She sniffed loudly, running her hands over her T-shirt and surreptitiously tucking it into her joggers. She wore her lucky Livin' on the Hedge undies. They had the cutest little hedgehogs printed all over them, with the words scrawled across her bottom. Her Aunt Suzi had given them to her before the older woman went bonkers.

Nope.

She would not think about that now. This was too important. Sammi had one last task before she received her diploma from the Academy, and she needed to focus. It was her last chance to show the instructors she could run the tactical obstacle course without causing a disaster. This was her last chance to pass.

Sammi had dreamed of becoming a FUC agent for most of her life. Aunt Suzi had been an inspiration to the young hedgie when she was just a hoglet. Being accepted to this super-intense program was one of her life's goals. Now, having achieved that, she simply had to graduate.

To the public, they were ARSHOL. It was short for *Animal Rescue Special House of Learning*, but to shifters and others who knew of the paranormal world, they were FUCN'A.

Nerves assailed her as Sammi tried to steady her pulse. She really wanted to become a FUC agent. To be a woman of mystery. To lead a life of danger and excitement.

Sniff.

Okay, maybe not danger. But excitement, sure! Aunt Suzi used to tell the most amazing stories of her daring deeds. But that was before the nasty stuff happened. Back when the older woman used to be Sammi's hero. Aunt Suzi was one hell of a FUC back then. At least, that was what Sammi's parents always said.

Of course, she wanted to follow in her footsteps. Who wouldn't?

The postcards her aunt used to send from faraway places had filled the young hoglet's head with fantastical daydreams. For most of her life, Sammi had prepared to attend FUCN'A. She studied hard, worked summer jobs to save up money, and read everything she could on espionage tactics. She was going to be a great FUC. Just like Aunt Suzi.

Of course, as the saying went, the best-laid plans of mice and men, *and hedgies*, often went awry. After the incident, everything changed. Not that she ever learned what the incident was exactly.

Still, poor Sammi had developed a little bitty case of anxiety with dangerous situations. As in *every situation* a FUC agent came across.

Sigh.

See, it all started when Aunt Suzi came to visit just after Sammi started her classes at FUCN'A. Sammi's mother's sister's last assignment was as a deep undercover agent infiltrating a tight-lipped group of feral cat shifters.

Like their wild relatives, some feline shifters tended to be haughty and of the opinion the entire world should bow down to them. Unfortunately, having a hedgehog as an ally did not go over too well with the extremists.

Once it was discovered Aunt Suzi was just another FUC, well, all hell had broken loose. Cover blown, she'd been treated to tortures the likes of which Sammi could hardly imagine.

All she knew was several of them had involved milk and, to a lactose intolerant hedgehog, the results were curdling.

After being rescued, the battered hedgie had been sent to Sammi's parents' house to recuperate from her ordeal. She'd received a medal for bravery and a commendation from her boss, but Sammi hardly thought it worth losing three toes and part of her left ear.

Physical scarring aside, it was the mental and emotional damage that truly scared Sammi. Aunt Suzi could not speak for weeks at first. She'd hardly ever come out of her room.

She was better now, barely, and still staying with the Andrews. Her bedroom was in the mother-in-law suite over the garage. Her window was adjacent to Sammi's room, so Sammi couldn't help but hear the woman's ramblings and nightmares. Aunt Suzi had taken an early retirement after refusing to leave the house.

"C-cats," she muttered often and non-stop. "Cats are every-

where. They see everything. Evil, evil, I tell you! Milk, only milk. That's all they drink. They want to rule. I am not going back, I tell you, I'm not. Just let them have it all! And they can keep their filthy milk too."

Sammi's parents simply laughed away Aunt Suzi's behavior, excusing it as just a case of overexcitement. They meant well, but Sammi was a bit more concerned. Would she lose her mind, too, if she became an agent? Would the danger prove too much?

So...okay. Maybe she was a coward. At least she would be alive *and sane*. Sane was the key word.

"Am I interrupting your personal vacation over there, Ms. Andrews?" Eliza Cogdill, assistant to the director of the Academy, pointed at Sammi with the hand that still held her ever-present smartphone.

The red-tailed chipmunk shifter chittered with her annoyance. She stepped into Samantha's personal space, frowning deeply at her. As if she could somehow make her move by sheer will.

As it was, Sammi's feet were glued to the floor. Even in the cute new sneakers she'd bought specifically to bolster her confidence, she found she simply could not move.

"I understand you've failed all of your other tactical training courses. This is your last chance to pass. Well? Move it, cadet!" Ms. Cogdill snapped her teeth closed aggressively for someone so small.

Sheesh. She sure was terrifying for a person of such minuscule stature. Not that Sammi should talk. At five-foot nothing, she was also considered a vertically challenged individual.

With more curves than was common for the average shifter, she'd heard all the slights and criticisms she cared to in her lifetime. Even tiny shifters like her hedgie didn't need to be reminded constantly of her less-than-impressive size. She did her best not to criticize others' physical appearances. After all, it was what was inside that counted.

Of course, what was inside Ms. Cogdill appeared to be as nasty as she was short. But maybe she just didn't like her.

Sniff.

Oh well. You can't make everyone happy. That was what her mom always said.

Sammi was at an important crossroads in her life. The firearms tactical training course was her last chance. The thing was Sammi would not be shooting guns this time around. Though her aim left something to be desired, she found her confidence much higher when she was standing behind an automatic.

This course was not about shooting. It was about ducking. As in, Sammi would be running and dodging bullets. And not in her cute new kicks, either. Nope. She would be doing all this in her other *spikier* and *smaller* skin.

"It is time. Now, run this course, cadet. FUC needs you!"

She nodded her head and took one step closer to the start of the training course. If she passed, that would mean she graduated from the Academy. Then Sammi would finally be eligible to serve all of shifter-kind as a FUC agent.

Mind made up, Sammi strode forward, praying like hell she could go through with it unscathed. After all, what were a few rounds of non-lethal ammo to a hedgehog? Their rounds weren't live, right? She wondered, suddenly unsure.

Gulp.

She dropped down onto all fours and shifted into her beastie. Hoping like hell her newly developed allergy to all things dangerous stayed far away from her for the moment. So, what if she'd gotten a little accident-prone these last few months?

If her tires went flat whenever she drove over forty miles per hour, it was a coincidence. If the store ran out of her favorite brand of cereal when she had a craving, that was okay. And if the electricity seemed to fritz whenever she plugged in her laptop in the library, well, how could it be her fault?

Sammi was not jinxed. Even if her hair spiked up whenever she smelled smoke or gunpowder. That was just a reaction. No big deal.

And her aversion to hand-to-hand combat after she'd accidentally put four of her fellow cadets in the hospital, subsequent to sticking them with her spines on account of them getting a little too rough with her softish self, was well-founded. Could anyone really blame her if she wasn't prepared to have her boobs and bottom assaulted in what she'd thought was a friendly sparring display?

Sniff.

She hardly thought the incident, or rather incidents, worthy of the terrible moniker her classmates had given her. Wedgie hedgie did not read well, no matter how you looked at it.

"Move it, Miss Andrews!" screamed Ms. Cogdill through her smartphone's megaphone app, and the world suddenly erupted into a cacophony of *bangs*, *booms*, *kapows*, and *yikeses*!

As if in slow motion, Sammi spied dozens of weapons firing at her from every direction. Behind each gun and arrow was the snarling face of one of her comrades-in-arms. Several from the aforementioned sparring class.

Oops.

It wasn't that she did not trust them not to harm her. It was just, *well*, she feared their intentions were not altogether peaceful.

As a result, Sammi panicked. Her hedgehog's feet, while small, were fast as she scurried across the uneven forest flooring that made up the training course.

She squeaked, ducking for cover as one arrow zipped straight across her tiny nose. Spines straightened as tall as they could go, she trembled violently as she ran.

Try as they might, her quills could not stop the incoming assault. Doing her best to dodge a spray of bullets that suspiciously appeared to be live ammo, Sammi ran straight into Melissa Olyphant's left calf. For some reason or other, the rhinoceros shifter was still in her human form, leaving her soft skin susceptible to the sharp quills on Sammi's back.

Her spines pierced the woman's leg, causing her to scream and flail her arms wildly, which sent one of the tall, thin flagpoles marking the course crashing toward the observation deck where Miss Cogdill stood.

4

Sammi ran faster. Conscious of her overreaction, yet unable to stop herself, her tiny feet flew over dirt, rocks, and patches of grass. Her hedgie's ears were hypersensitive to the sounds of bullets flying, training grenades exploding, dirt spraying, people shouting, and all the chaos that followed her faux pas.

Her hedgie's heart was beating a bazillion times a second, but when she finally made it through all forty yards without further incident, Sammi was relieved. She shifted back to her human skin, quickly donning one of the several robes waiting at the end of the course.

Then she blinked. *Uh-oh.* Looking around at the broken, busted training course and the several moaning and groaning shifters could mean only one thing. She was getting a big fat F.

Sigh.

Sammi could not believe her eyes. Miss Cogdill was on a stretcher, having been hit in the head with the flagpole. Melissa, the rhino, was in one beside her, on her side. She was wailing in pain, with an estimated dozen of Samantha's sharp needle-like spines sticking out of the back of her leg.

The students who'd been firing on her all seemed to suffer from some kind of mishap or other. Their weapons had developed a malfunction or ten after firing on Sammi. It seemed some guns jammed. One bow was strung too tight, and the arrow wound up going backward, impaling the archer. Other guns backfired, and one grenade imploded before the tosser tossed it.

Gulp.

Ironically, after a few days, Sammi got some good news. She passed the course. Not with an A, but a pass was a pass in her book.

No one could blame Sammi for what had happened. At least not directly. So, what if she had a little allergy to violence? Everyone had their own strengths and weaknesses. She was eligible for full FUC duty.

But after waiting several weeks with no placement offers under any Furry United Coalition mentor agents, Sammi had no choice but to accept she'd blown it. She tried not to feel disappointed. But how could she not?

Sammi had made a mess of things.

Present-day at the Academy...

"Well?"

"Well, what?" Sammi was looking over online job listings. If she wasn't going to be able to fulfill her two-year commitment to FUC, she'd have to get a job fast to pay back her training.

"Earth to Samantha! I mean, *hello*, I am trying to talk to

you," Sofia Leeds, *formerly Pelosi*, dropped her biodegradable fork in exasperation.

Uhoh.

Sammi must have missed something important. The chinchilla shifter would never voluntarily put down her fork when she had a plate of Maude's meatless meatballs sitting in front of her. Sweet marinara sauce on the side, the delectable vegetarian delights were tempting even to an omnivore like Sammi.

Technically, it was *Tofu Taco Tuesday*, but Maude always seemed to keep a stash of the little fried goodies on hand whenever Sofia was there. Her chinchilla friend got special treatment from the hare shifter whenever she was on campus and in the cafeteria. Which was often these days.

Come to think of it, Sofia looked a little bit rounder and softer these days. Sammi scratched her head, sighing aloud when she came across a lock of her thick hair sticking up in wild disarray. Her dark locks tended to mimic her spiny beastie's quills, and though she tried extra hard to tame them, it was a losing battle.

"Um, Sof, why all the meatballs?" she asked gently.

"Duh, Sammi. I am pregnant. Which brings me to the point of this lunch."

"Really? Congrats," she screeched then faked a frown. "So, wait a minute. You didn't just wanna hang out and see if I could scarf down ten of Maude's tofu tacos without puking?"

"OMFG, shut up. You will so puke." Sofia laughed. "Seriously, Tony wants me to really take care of myself during this pregnancy, so I am thinking of taking a leave of absence. Well? What do you think?" Sofia asked, and it was obvious her bestie was repeating herself.

Oops. Sniff.

Hedgehogs were well known for their tendency to pick up emotions in the scents of others. Her own sow was ciphering through the myriad of flavors to gauge Sofia's emotions. Judging from the citrusy tang in her usually sweet smell, Sofia was annoyed.

"Uh, did I already say congrats?"

"Yes, Samantha." Sofia tsked. "You know, ever since the first day you walked into my office as a young cadet needing my guidance, I knew there was something special about you," she said, but her eyes kept straying to the top of Samantha's head.

"It's my hair, isn't it?"

"No, no. Um, okay. Yes, but just a little bit. Here." Sofia blushed. "Uh, sorry. You just got a little..." The chinchilla shifter leaned forward as far as her gently protruding belly would allow, and to Samantha's horror, Sofia licked her hand, using the flat of it to try to pat down Sammi's spikes. "Uh, okay, well, that is a bit better."

"Did you just mom-lick me?" Sammi whispered, shocked by the occurrence.

"Um, yes?"

"First, I get denied a car loan for some secondhand sedan that wasn't even anywhere near my dream car, but I thought I could afford it, and now this? A mom-lick? In public, Sof? Ugh." Sammi's eyes widened at her friend's actions.

Sniff. Oh, the humiliation!

She'd just been treated to a quick spit-fix from her bestie. Is this what her life had become? Her inner hedgie shivered at the thought. It was unimaginable. Her beautiful spines were meant to poke and defy gravity.

True. But she would rather her hair not mimic the

deadly little *pointies*. An unfortunate side effect of being a hedgehog shifter with a short fuse to full-on panic mode.

Sigh.

"Um, yeah, okay. I think I overstepped. I apologize." Sofia blushed a furious shade of pink before clearing her throat. "Anyway, Sammi, the point is I think you would be great."

"At what?"

"At my job. I am going to recommend you as my temporary fill-in."

"Wait, what?"

"Look, you said yourself being a FUC agent isn't all it's cracked up to be," Sofia said with kindness shining in her eyes. "Maybe helping cadets *be all they can be* is more your speed." She nodded.

"Oh, I never considered—"

"Well, then start," Sofia said sternly. "This way, you're still working for FUC, so you don't have to pay back your training and allowance. Besides, I know you are going to be the best Conflict Resolution & Situation De-escalation Counselor FUCN'A has ever seen!"

"I am?" *Sniff.* "Yes, I am!"

5

PRIC Headquarters, New Jersey

Twenty-four hours after the explosion where Julietta DiCarlo was rescued...

Sergio was still at his desk at PRIC headquarters, filling out forms and updating the inter-agency task force on what went down at the warehouse that day.

For shits and giggles, he also added in his current progress on the identity thief and how he believed it might tie into their other case. They had to be connected. He felt it in his gut.

He was in the process of plotting out the timeline of events, as far as he knew them, when he was interrupted. The sound of Italian leather loafers and the scent of fresh cannoli cream reached him.

Holy mother of cheesy pastry goodness.

Sergio sniffed the air, and his stomach growled. Damn, that smelled good.

"What's doin', Serg?" Tony Leeds approached with a

white pastry box that looked suspiciously like it came from *Bear Claw Bakery*.

The man wore his usual black-on-black getup with a shit-eating grin that told of his recently found happiness.

Looks good on him, Sergio admitted to himself and wondered what brought on such a positive change in his coworker's demeanor. His interest was fleeting, however, in favor of more important things. Like his growling stomach.

Far as he knew, the world-famous bakery did not make Italian pastries, and yet... He was definitely not mistaken. The subtle scent of sweetened *impastata ricotta* perfumed with the zests of fresh lemons and oranges, mixed with miniature chocolate chips was indisputable.

Sweet heaven. He was practically drooling on his paperwork. A bull his size needed to eat regularly to keep his energy up, and he'd run out of carrots hours ago.

Grrr. This time the growling noise was from his stomach, not his bull.

Sigh. How embarrassing.

"Tony." He nodded, eyes on the box that he now knew bore the Bear Claw Bakery's world-famous logo.

Gulp. The goodies were so close. And yet, just out of reach.

"I came to see you personally, my friend, to bring you a token of my thanks." Tony placed the box on Sergio's desk.

Sergio's bull growled happily. Or was that his stomach again? Either way, he was two seconds away from ripping into the cardboard, or maybe just chewing through it. But manners, which had been beaten into his thick head by Grandpa Sal with many a wooden spoon, dictated he say thank you first.

Sad moo.

"No need to thank me," Sergio said, though he accepted

Tony's hand, shaking it briefly, before turning his attention to the delectable goodies.

Damn. He was starved. Patience gone, he ripped open the box and groaned aloud. Six of the hefty-sized delicacies sat inside.

"Holy shit, they're cannoli-cream-filled bear claws!"

His voice was laced with awe. But how could it not be? Such culinary delights as this deserved to be applauded.

Happy moo.

He sighed, and yeah, a little bit of drool might have actually escaped his lips this time around.

"Yeah." Tony grinned. "They're doing them up now after I made a little request for the reception Grandmother Leeds gave us last month. Calling them *Tony's Special*," he added proudly. "I missed seeing you there."

"Oh." Sergio grimaced, stopping with the first bear claw halfway to his mouth, to the infinite sorrow of his stomach. "Sorry, man. I was on a case."

"Figured as much. No worries." Tony exhaled. "You found my sister, and for that, I am eternally grateful. By the way, this is my wife and mate, Sofia," he said, introducing the small female who joined them.

The curly-haired woman walked directly to his side with a contented smile on her face.

Sergio grimaced. He loathed having to pause in his attempt to scarf down the pastry once again, but it was necessary. Polite smile in place, he wiped his hand hastily on his shirt before shaking hers.

"Ma'am." He tried to hold on to his smile, but he really, *really* wanted to eat the sweet-smelling, drool-worthy pastry. Like now.

"Sergio, right? It is so nice to meet you." She nodded.

"Thank you so much for rescuing my sister-in-law. I was just on the phone with her, and she was asking for you."

"Oh. Nice kid. I'm glad she's okay," he murmured half-heartedly.

Was the entire world conspiring to stop him from indulging in the sweet treat? But he knew better than to express his grief. Sergio just nodded again and complimented the couple.

Yes, he had manners. Contrary to popular belief, growing up on a farm did not mean you were an animal.

Snort.

"You can't imagine how worried we've been." Tony sucked in a breath to hide the depth of his feelings. "We were so relieved when news came that you found her. This is personal for me, *bruthah*," he added, Tony's Jersey accent changing the word brother as only natives of the Garden State could, to Sergio's utter amusement.

"SCARAB is responsible for a lot of harm."

"Indeed, *bruthah*," Sergio agreed.

His lips quirked at their exchange. It never ceased to amaze him how thick his accent got when talking to a fellow Jersey boy. They tended to drop the *r* at the end of words, while adding an *ah* kinda sound.

So, brother became *bruthah*, water became *wawtah*, and so on. Sergio himself was guilty of similar verbal intonations. And he was even known to favor colloquialisms.

6

There was only one stereotype he hated, and that was the notion that people from New Jersey called it *New Joizy*. No Garden State native said that. Not ever. And if someone tried to claim they did, well then, his bull was more than happy to set them straight.

Grrr. This is one proud Jersey bull, bitches.

"I am sorry for that, Tony. I'm real glad she's safe now," Sergio added.

"Sofia and I were still in Vegas. You know, *honeymoonin'*. The ink wasn't even dry on our marriage license when we got the news. Fuckers nabbed Julietta right in a public parking lot." He shook his head, and anger turned his face red.

For a moment, Sergio worried that shit was about to hit the fan. Then Tony's wife pressed closer to his side, and the man's beast seemed to ebb with the pressure.

"Tony, it's not your fault," she whispered.

Sergio dropped the pastry back into the box. He could eat later. Besides, he fully empathized with the relief etched on Tony's face now that his sister was safe and sound. But more curious to the bull was the way his peer held the small, curly-haired woman close to him.

They looked complete in a way his bullish heart had never expected to witness. As if she were born to be at the man's side. Two halves of a whole. Sergio nodded, but his heart squeezed enviously. That shared look on their faces told him everything he needed to know about the situation.

The rumors were true. Tony Leeds had found his *fated mate* while visiting the Furry United Coalition Academy, or *FUCN'A* as it was known—the *N* being for *newbies*.

Even Tony Leeds, Jersey Devil, and womanizer extraordinaire, has a fated mate, thought Sergio, with no negligible amount of astonishment.

She was so much tinier than the broad-shouldered, dark-haired man. Her head barely touched his chin. But she seemed neither afraid nor reluctant. Astonishing. Was that truly how these things worked?

Opposites attract. That was what people said. Looking down at his own incredible size, Sergio shook his head. He sure as fuck hoped that saying was true. Otherwise, he'd be mated to a Mack truck.

Snort.

Didn't matter. Not really. As long as his mate was someone who loved him, Sergio didn't care what she looked like. He'd just recently started feeling his years and the loneliness that accompanied being a PRIC.

Sad moo.

"I know, doll face, but she's my kid *sistah*. I feel responsible. Don't matter now though, huh? This big lug found her. She's safe now, ain't she?" Tony said, interrupting Sergio's thoughts.

He watched the man lean down to nuzzle his mate's cheek, dropping a soft, gentle kiss on her lips. Lucky SOB.

Sergio felt his face heat. He turned away to give them a little privacy. He was starting to feel like a creep for spying on the couple. Looking down instead, he exhaled.

The breathing courses did come in handy now and then, he assured himself. Waiting a beat before facing the newlyweds once again, he immediately noticed something odd in the way Sofia kept a protective hand over her stomach.

Holy crap.

Realization dawned, and his bull snorted once more. He didn't need to be a detective to realize she was expecting. Shifter pregnancies were always a cause for celebration, but Sergio would keep that to himself until they offered to share their news.

Farm needs young to keep it going. Someday, he thought to himself. *Maybe someday soon*, his bull hoped.

Being near the two of them, so happy and in love, only seemed to make his own solitary state that much more glaring.

Shit.

He wasn't thinking about finding his own mate. Not for years yet. Right? No way. He had too much on his plate to worry about that.

Grrrr.

Unfortunately for Sergio, his bull did not quite agree. His inner animal was tired of his self-proclaimed grazing habits. He wanted a mate of his own.

Double shit.

"Well, uh, thanks for dropping by. And like I said, this was all completely unnecessary, but appreciated." He stood up, ready to escort the happy couple right out the door.

The two lovebirds were contagious insofar as making his usually peaceful inner bull a raging maniac looking for love. Sergio was not interested. Period.

Best he stayed far away from mated couples for a while. At least until this sudden surge of hormones was over.

"Nah, Sergio," Tony said, gripping his shoulder with a surprisingly strong hand. "Of course, I need to thank you. You saved my sister, and now you're family."

"Uh, yeah, okay. I appreciate that, Tony, but I am sure you and the missus have better things to do—"

"Yeah, we were on our way back to visit Julietta."

"She still in the HOLE?"

"Yeah. This Dr. Finn says he needs to do more cognitive tests."

"I see. Well, good luck with that."

"Say, did you ever figure out how your identity theft was related to this kidnapping? I mean I'm sure this is SCARAB. Crime scene photos showed the same beetle etched into the cornerstone outside the warehouse."

Tony's devil peeked through his reddening eyes, and Sergio figured he could share *some* of what he knew with his fellow PRIC.

"You know, I can't divulge what I've learned in an ongoing investigation." Sergio shook his head. "But I will say this. I have an idea brewing. Soon as I follow up on some solid leads, it will only be a matter of time."

"Fair enough." Tony squinted.

"Sorry I have no more info for you, Tony," he said.

"Nah, I get it. You're a good PRIC to have around, Serg."

7

One thing Sergio didn't fuck around with, and that was the rules. No detective working for PRIC ever got away with bending the regulations and directives.

Except for Tony. But now everyone knew he was the boss' grandson. Some griped, but not Sergio. He didn't have two shits to give either way. Tony could do whatever Tony liked, and Sergio would keep doing what he liked. Long as he toed the line and got results.

He always did like rules. They were neat and tidy.

"Tell you what, Sergio." Tony turned back to face him. "I'm not sure if you heard, but I opened a field office up in Canada. Just a little PRIC headquarters up north. If you ever need a change of scenery, make sure you come see me. Anytime you want, *bruthah*."

"Sweet," Sergio replied. "Thank you for the offer, Tony. I might take you up on that."

After the happy couple left, and his bull settled down, Sergio looked over his completed timeline and grabbed the pastry that had been evading consumption.

Mmmm. The first bite was pure bliss. *Now, where was I? Oh yeah.*

He'd been called in to investigate the misuse of Bernadine Spirito's granddaughter's identity a couple of months ago. Through that investigation, he'd discovered the five other cases that resemble the Spirito identity theft—including the one involving the missing gopher shifter, Samantha Andrews, and her grandmother.

Julietta DiCarlo, mouse shifter, had been abducted roughly twenty-eight days after he'd started working the case. Nothing new or striking there.

The tip that came in earlier was odd. Sergio had been next up, so he'd gotten the gig. The anonymous tipster had reported suspicious activity in an abandoned warehouse and alluded to more substantial evidence on-site. He also made a vague statement about *not following the money.*

Nothing special about that, but the caller had used the special PRIC tipster hotline, only known in shifter circles. It guaranteed the crime was related to the supernatural world.

Once the human authorities were circumvented, Sergio headed out to investigate and came upon the raging multi-building fire. He called into the proper authorities, and despite the firefighters' warnings to stay out until they had the blaze under control, he investigated the building. And was glad he had; otherwise, he might not have found Tony's sister.

But what does that have to do with stolen identities and bank accounts?

Julietta DiCarlo had been kidnapped. Her identity had not been hacked. A look into her finances showed no unusual activity. He was at a dead end.

He wasn't sure how the two tied together or why they

did, but there was definitely some overlapping. It could not be mere coincidence. He felt it in his gut.

"Gotta find the tie-in, Sergio," he grumbled to himself.

Talking to himself was part of his process. Kept him honest, or at least that was how he figured it. Same as his Grandpa Sal had taught him.

After all, an honest man had to start telling the truth somewhere, and that was best often kept to himself. Grandpa Sal had lots of useful information like that. Came from his rather colorful past.

The Gravinos had an unusual history. His family tree thrived under a heavy amount of shade in its early days in the good ol' USA. A little more than he'd have liked to admit. In all honesty, they had questionable associations and, in some cases, relationships with known criminals, but the end result was all that counted.

The Gravinos had made good on their business goals. Going completely legit long before Sergio was born. The rest simply was whatever it was.

What it all added up to now was Sergio Gravino never told a lie. He was proud of his heritage, despite the illegal undertones that colored parts of it. If being honest proved too difficult, well, he learned to simply stay quiet.

Some thought the Gravino organization was still a major player in the underground shifter world, but as far as he knew, they had been out of that business for years.

Beets, carrots, and cabbages were the Gravino family's stock in trade these days. The farm his grandfather ran was large and state-of-the-art. A real tribute to non-GMO, organic growers in the Garden State.

Sure, they had some visitors from the old days, but they were just friends. Grandpa Sal assured him their holdings were strictly on the up and up these days. It would not do well for the older bull to be involved in anything criminal. Not with a grandson who was a detective.

At any rate, Sergio had been vetted thoroughly before coming to work for PRIC. And now, he was hot on the trail of one of the most heinous organizations out there. Stealing identities was despicable. Ruining someone else's hard-earned life for the sake of a few baubles was indefensible.

But experimenting on shifters, as the organization known as SCARAB was known to do, was about the evilest thing he had ever heard. Immoral, unethical, vile, and truly heinous.

Were the two cases intertwined? Sergio could not prove it yet, but he sure as hell thought so.

The task force assigned to locating and ending SCARAB's nefarious deeds was a far cry from his little identity theft ring. Still, something about what the tipster had said when he called in the location where Ms. DiCarlo was being kept bugged him.

Something about warning the detectives to not follow the money. What money? Why mention money? Why set the fire if not to cover something up? All good questions. All begging answers he did not have. Yet. The key word was *yet*.

He needed to go over that recording again. One quick email to Joe Canary had Sergio growling in his seat. Seemed the little birdy couldn't locate the message.

In fact, all traces were gone, except for the phone number. Interestingly enough, the phone, a burner that was now dead, had a Canadian area code.

"Very interesting," he mumbled to himself.

So what did he know? Well, Julietta DiCarlo was safe. Thank goodness.

But Bernadine Spirito's granddaughter's credit was not.

In fact, new activity was very troubling. The thief had somehow been approved for a $117,632 loan.

An oddly specific amount if Sergio ever saw one. Even worse, the thief received it in a wire transfer that went straight into an offshore account and was immediately converted to untraceable cryptocurrency.

Shit. It would be impossible to find.

"Another dead end," he growled to himself.

Another couple of hours zoomed by with Sergio hunkered down at his desk. His stomach growled and his back ached.

Just a few more minutes, he told himself. At least he still had snacks. Sighing, he reached for another delectable cannoli-cream-filled bear claw, but Sergio's searching hand encountered none. Only the empty bottom of the cardboard pastry box Tony Leeds had brought him.

Mournful moo.

"Are you still here, Mr. Gravino?"

He looked up swiftly from the empty box and cleared his throat at the untimely interruption.

Crap. His eyes landed on the formidable stare of one Margot Leeds. Sergio stood up too quickly, knocking down some of the files he'd borrowed from storage.

"Mrs. Leeds," he yelped, blushing furiously at the sound. "Yes, ma'am. Sorry. Uh, I was just—"

"No need to stumble over yourself, dear boy." His boss smiled, her white teeth gleaming sharply in the dim office light.

He had to wonder if the rumors were true about Jersey Devils. Predators were common in his world, but Jersey Devils were not.

They were a cryptozoid unknown to many. Rumored to be the result of an experimentation gone awry by the very same group PRICs like Tony Leeds were hunting to this day. Still, cannibalism was not an easy reputation to either earn or overcome.

Should the shifter in question want to do so, that is. Some preferred to keep others on their toes, wondering where the truth and fiction began.

Sergio had heard plenty about shifter families with infamous recipes used in celebration after defeating their enemies. Not that he was judging. With his family tree, how could he? Blood thirst was not reserved for carnivores alone. Take it from a vegetarian.

Why, his own great-grandfather, Salvatore Gravino, was said to possess a recipe for fertilizer that incorporated the siphoned marrow from his enemies' bones along with a hearty blend of entrails and organs.

Perfect for his various vegetable fields, in particular the beets, which always seemed sweeter afterward. Even better for Gravino Farms' blueberries.

8

The proof was in the pie. At least that was what Aunt Edith said. And her pies were the best. Baked daily during the season with the freshest Jersey blueberries, peaches, and apples. She even made a damn fine strawberry-rhubarb.

Yum.

Grandpa Sal had won the *Garden State Best Growers' Award* twenty years in a row. Coincidentally, his neighbor, a sheep shifter named Ted Logan, had not been seen since 1987.

The unfortunate man had lodged a complaint about noise pollution, blaming Grandpa Sal's tractor just a month before his disappearance.

He was a mean old fucker if memory served. Never returned any of Sergio's soccer balls when he'd accidentally kicked them over the fence dividing the two properties.

Asshat.

On the plus side, Grandpa Sal grew one hell of a crop. His tomatoes were the best. Oh, Sergio had absolutely loved the summers he spent on that farm. His grandfather grew the biggest, best veggies in the whole Garden state. So much so, Gravino Farms was one of the top produce exporters in all New Jersey.

The Garden State was, of course, renowned as a top produce exporter in the USA. One of the leading producers of cranberries, blueberries, eggplant, asparagus, and of course, tomatoes.

"Mr. Gravino?"

"What? Oh, sorry," he said, snapping back to reality. "Ma'am? Can I help you?"

"No, son." She grinned again. "I am here to help you. I understand the criminal responsible for stealing the Spirito granddaughter's identity is somehow linked to SCARAB?"

"It is a possibility, ma'am. Investigators have found the image of a beetle carved into the cornerstone of the warehouse where Ms. DiCarlo was being held. But the tip came into our hotline, not FUCs."

"Yes, I know. However, they also recovered this from the debris." She handed him a file folder, and he immediately opened it. "I had them scan the remnants of documents found on the site. These are copies. As you can see, the fire started in this room here. They were using it as an office. Those papers appear to be forgeries of official documents. The last one bears a name..."

"Spirito," he murmured, holding the paper that connected the dots.

His identity thief was in fact working for SCARAB. The evidence was right in front of him.

Grrr.

"Yes, it seems even criminal conspiracies like SCARAB need funding."

"I want in on this case, Mrs. Leeds," he grunted.

"I thought you would." She handed him an envelope. "I

take it you noticed the seal on the Spirito forged document?"

"It's from Service BC. That's where you get important documents like birth certificates and drivers' licenses in British Columbia—one of the provinces in Canada, right?"

"That's right."

"What's in the envelope, ma'am?"

"Your tickets, Mr. Gravino. I am making you the Detective in Charge of this case as far as PRIC is concerned." She smiled and added, "I believe my grandson offered you a place to stay. The plane leaves in a few hours. I suggest you take a shower and pack a bag."

Sergio nodded. Excitement thrummed through his veins at the very idea.

Holy shit.

His years of good, old-fashioned, honest, hard work were finally paying off. Every PRIC dreamed of heading his own case, and he was no different. His bull grunted in anticipation of the upcoming hunt, and Sergio pushed the pedal to the metal, practically flying home in his SUV.

Packing his travel case took precious minutes, but he finished and headed for the door. His stomach growled, but he pushed his hunger aside. This was no time to get his chow on.

Sergio was a DIC now. And he had a thief to catch.

9

Sergio exited the taxi and took in the surrounding area.

Whoa. Canada sure is pretty, he thought as his big brown eyes focused in on the tidy little main street of the small town just outside of the Academy's campus grounds.

Playing the tourist wasn't too bad. Hell, at least it disguised his need to survey the area for any tails or signs of wrongdoing. Tony was late picking him up, but that was okay, too. Gave him more time for a little reconnaissance.

Stopping at the diner, he got himself a large garden salad with a light lemon vinaigrette. Next, he grabbed a tall iced coffee and waited on a park bench for his ride.

He didn't have to wait long. Tony pulled up in a shiny, sleek devil red Pontiac Trans Am with the *t-tops* off and Bon Jovi blasting. Sergio was a Boss man himself.

"*Bruthah*!" yelled the man with the devilish grin.

"Nice ride." Sergio smirked, shaking his head.

The guy never could do anything small or indiscreet. And he was supposed to be Sergio's cover. *SMH.* He snorted, but grinned all the same.

His bull was in a very good mood. *Must be the mountain*

air, he mused. After he'd finished his coffee, he did some breathing exercises to settle his chakra. Officially, Sergio was on vacation, visiting his buddy and new wife in the Rockies.

Unofficially, he was on assignment. Looking to prove the connection between Tony's sister's kidnapping and the identity thief who'd been plaguing one shifter child and at least five college-aged students in the United States—including Samantha Andrews, the gopher shifter who'd last been thought to be heading to FUCN'A.

Something tied them together, but the other agents and detectives on the SCARAB task force were not keen on his take of the whole operation. His boss had cleared the way for him to travel to Canada to follow his hunch.

Naming him the *Detective in Charge* of his own assignment. He was humbled by her steady belief in his investigative skills, even if she was only doing it for the sake of her grandson. After all, Julietta, the girl who'd been kidnapped, was Tony's adoptive sister.

Sergio had spent the entire airplane ride going through the files of the six victims of the identity thief he'd discovered thus far, but nothing linked them. At least not yet.

"So, Grandmother Leeds tells me she made you head DIC of this operation. Congrats, man! You have a line on one of your identity theft victims?"

Sergio was a little cramped in the sports car, but he managed to get his seatbelt on, having stored his travel bags behind him. He listened to the inquiry, considering it before he answered.

"Thanks, and yes. A gopher shifter named Samantha Andrews filed a report after strange accounts began to appear on her credit history. Clever girl was taking accounting classes before heading up here to FUCN'A for classes. According to her grandmother's bingo friends, she'd always dreamed of being an agent. But she headed to BC with her grandmother and then they both went incommunicado—no one has heard from either of them in the past eighteen months."

"I see." Tony nodded. "Lots of hopefuls come here to find out they can't hack it. My little *pasticcino* helped plenty of young shifters adjust to the Academy. You know she was a conflict resolution counselor."

"Yes, I heard. But what do you mean *was*?"

"Didn't I tell you? We're expecting our first." He grinned from ear to ear as he hooked a turn that had Sergio scrambling to hold on to his files.

"Yes, I figured that out the other day. Congratulations to you both," the bull said while he straightened his papers and shoved them back into his briefcase where it was safe.

"Come on, you can tell her yourself." Tony winked and pulled off the road into a complex of little townhouses.

"I figured you'd need your own space, so I went ahead and grabbed you the vacant unit across from ours for a few weeks." Tony pointed to a decent-sized townhouse directly across the paved walkway from where the Jersey Devil and his mate resided.

"The people who live there are on a tour of Europe and were going to list it on some vacation swap site, but I told them I'd do them one better. Fridge is stocked, and there's a cleaning lady that comes over on Wednesdays."

"Thank you," Sergio said.

Sure, I'm a Jersey boy, er, bull, but I could graze around here for hours.

His bull snorted happily as Sergio's eyes wandered across the neat little complex that sat snuggly against a stand of pines that broke away into a protected forest area.

He took in a cleansing breath of fresh mountain air. Yes,

indeed, his beast was right. He was a Jersey boy at heart, but Canada was sweet. Lots of open spaces, forests to explore, and plenty of fresh, clean air to breathe.

He tried not to notice as Sofia came outside and embraced her husband lovingly. Imagine coming home to someone like that. Someone waiting just for you.

Silly romantic idea for sure, but dammit, his bull yearned for a mate. And he'd been ignoring that yearning for too long, it seemed.

Sad moo.

He bypassed the still clinging couple and dropped off his things at his rented townhouse, the key to which was under the mat, before heading back over.

So trusting, he mused, slipping the metal fob into his pocket. Back in Jersey, he sure as shit would never leave a key under the mat. He counted to ten, wanting to give the couple ample time to say their hellos.

10

His bull was anxious enough without having a reminder that others were happily mated while he was still *very single* thrust in his face.

Hell, I'm practically a confirmed bachelor.

Sad moo.

Tony was surprisingly thoughtful, renting a fully furnished townhouse for him. He wouldn't have to worry about fixing the place up or have to deal with scratchy hotel sheets. The inferior thread counts did terrible things to his skin.

Happy snort.

After dropping off his luggage and briefcase, he walked back over to Tony's to come up with a game plan. The two lovebirds were still snug, sitting close on the couch, cuddling. His bull pushed against his skin, but he wrestled the beast down. That kind of life just wasn't in the cards for him.

Angry grunt.

"I thought you were gonna nap, baby doll? Traveling back and forth wore you out," Tony said to Sofia, nuzzling her neck, and wrapping her up in a tight hug. "You promised."

"I was, but I had a lunch date with Sammi."

"That was today?"

"Uh-huh." She kissed her mate's chin, and Sergio felt very much like a peeping bull.

"Uh, excuse me," he interrupted.

He felt odd standing in the doorway, unintentionally eavesdropping. Tony growled, skin reddening with his inner beast. Ducking his head, Sergio waited for Tony's devil to recede. The man's semi-shift was lightning fast and impressive as all hell. Once his skin became flesh-colored again, Sergio walked inside.

"Sorry about that, Sergio. Tony's got a hair-trigger temper ever since we found out about junior," Sofia explained, leaving a possessive hand on her husband's arm.

Sergio's interrupting them caused the mated male to get a little bit grumpy. It was a shifter thing. "I understand." He nodded, even though he didn't.

Sadness filled him. He supposed he never would feel that way. Protective and possessive over both mate and young. Tony was blessed.

We will be too. When we meet our mate.

Nope. Not happening for us. We have our work.

Mournful moo.

He ignored his brazen bovine's bawling for a mate. The silly bull needed to keep his eye on the target. Which was to catch this rotten crook or crooks before they hurt someone.

"I made a timeline of events." He handed Tony the document he'd been working on over the past few hours.

"As you can see, the identity thief seems to be working with no real pattern. Each of these victims had strange charges on their accounts as early as months before the big loans hit their credit reports, but none of them seemed to notice until it was too late. Each one taken for hundreds of thousands of dollars."

"And you spoke to all of them?"

"All except two. Spirito is a minor so I only spoke to her legal guardian—her grandmother, Bernadine Spirito. And the other is the missing gopher shifter—all records indicate she and her grandmother should be here."

Of course, when Sergio said here, it was more like *heeyah*. That Jersey accent was a killer, but Tony had the same one. Worse even, given the devil's predilection for Italian American slang as a result of being raised by his adoptive parents. Italian Americans from Philly were hard-core AF.

"Here?" repeated Tony.

"That's what I said, *bruthah*."

"A'ight."

Snort. Yep. Jersey sure is in da house.

"FUCN'A," he replied, cocky grin and all.

"You've been waiting a while to say that, haven't you?" Sofia sighed.

"Yep." Sergio nodded.

And why not? It was a good one too. If he did say so himself.

"All right, well, you two can speak your native tongue while I go have that lie-down."

"You okay, doll?"

"Of course." She smiled at Tony. "Oh, and Sergio, feel free to use my car if you like. I will be in the rest of the night."

"Thanks. I just might do that. See you guys later."

Sergio was anxious to check out his first lead. Yeah, he should wait, but what for? He was raring to go.

11

Sammi looked at the large clock hanging on the wall of her new office digs. It was her first day on the job, and she felt as if she'd been hit over the head with a baseball bat.

Who knew cadets could be so extra? She turned her waning attention back on the shifter who'd rushed to her desk almost immediately that morning.

It had been hours now, and the poor creature was still going on and on. Sammi was doing her best to follow along. But it wasn't easy.

"The last counselor I worked with always looked at me when I was talking," the young cadet complained.

"Uh, sorry." Sammi redirected her gaze to the female and nodded for her to continue.

"All right then. So, anyway, then I woke up, and everything was gone! All her clothes, books, and her half of the toiletries. Plus, that rat ate all my cheese spray," Randee, a raccoon shifter who seemed to have an unhealthy affinity for eyeliner and cheese spray, wailed.

It seemed her roommate had bailed on her without so much as a word. If this conversation was anything to go by, she probably would not have been able to get a word in anyway.

"Did you try listening to her before things escalated to this point?"

"Are you saying this is my fault?" Randee screeched, causing many pairs of eyes to gaze harshly at Sammi.

The raccoon shifter's face scrunched up. A warning sign if ever there was one. Then she proceeded to bawl all over Sammi's desk.

Dang it.

"No, no, no." Sammi tried to reason. "I'm sorry, Randee, that was not what I meant at all. How about a tissue?"

"Is my makeup smudged?"

"No, well, maybe a little." Sammi scrambled for some wipes she saw in the desk drawer and handed them to the female, who admittedly looked more like her animal half with black makeup smeared all over her eyes.

Great job, Sammi. Sniff.

She tried to act like everything was fine. But so far, day one of her new life sucked balls. The big, hairy, sweaty kind.

When Sofia asked her to take over her position as her first official FUC assignment, Sammi had no idea it would be *this*.

Sniff.

This position was a far cry from an actual FUC field agent gig. Instead of chasing bad guys, she babysat cadets all day long. It was tedious. And awful. *Like really awful.* And Sammi was bad at it. Would the whining never stop? Or the sniveling excuses?

Nope.

What did these people even have to complain about? They were specially chosen out of thousands of applicants.

Cream of the crop. Literally, at the top of their fields, from various subgroups of shifters.

Sammi was proud she'd even made it as far as the front door. Thank goodness for her avid reading habits. Her ability to remember things she'd read was what landed her the spot at FUCN'A.

But back to Miss Messy Eyeliner here. So, her roommate switched rooms. *BFD.*

Did Randee send Director Cooper's assistant to the emergency room? Was she asked to take her final tactical exams three separate times to pass?

Nope.

Not as far as Sammi knew.

And last, did she earn the horrible nickname "*wedgie hedgie*" by the staff and faculty?

Sad sniff. That honor was reserved for Sammi alone. At first, she didn't even get it. She'd thought perhaps her underwear had peeked through the top of her pants or something. But of course, that wasn't why she'd been given the moniker.

Apparently, Sammi had been named the "wedgie hedgie" because every time she showed up for class or a tactical lesson, her instructor's glutes clenched tight in fear wreaking all sorts of havoc with their tighty-whities.

Yep. Humiliations galore was apparently the new theme of her life.

Sammi had the privilege of being the only FUCN'A grad in the history of the Academy who'd achieved every single one of those underwhelming feats she'd named.

Maybe if she'd stop picturing images of her Aunt Suzi climbing the curtains to get away from imaginary feral cats, she could've done more at FUCN'A. As it was, she'd not been offered a mentorship, and she was essentially doomed to office work.

Sad sniff.

"Uh, Randee?"

The raccoon was occupying too much space at her desk. Her tiny body was sprawled over half of it, and it was clear she was going through some serious emotional turmoil.

Sammi had no idea how to deal with it. Her hedgie's sensitive snout was picking up all sorts of crazy from the female.

Sigh. This is my life now.

"Okay, Randee, I am going to get you some more tissues. Then I need you to fill out this paperwork in response to your roommate's COC forms, so we can all find an amenable solution, okay? One minute." She excused herself and headed over to Tammy's desk.

12

The older woman was tall and thin. A squirrel shifter, who Sofia had recommended to her should she need help. It was true too. Tammy was the most helpful person Sammi had ever met.

"What can I do you for, Miss Sammi?" she asked with her usual chipper disposition.

Sammi's nose twitched in reaction. As if the other shifter's happiness had set off one of her notorious allergic responses. She closed her eyes, but it was no good. Her hair had already started feathering out. An echo of her beastie's spines.

Sigh.

"Where can I find the right paperwork for a cadet to fill out in response to a COC form?"

"The complainant's COC was filed against your cadet?"

"Yes. They were roommates, but the complainant stated irreconcilable differences on her form as the reason for needing to switch rooms."

Her face must have shown some of her displeasure and

weariness over the whole thing. Tammy tsked and patted her hand.

"You okay, hon?"

"I swear I did not know this was what this job entailed."

"I understand. It can be difficult. Now"—Tammy nodded—"what you need is a *harder cock.*"

"A what?" Sammi's mouth hung wide open, and she noted a few snorts in the area.

"I said you need a *harder cock*," the skinny squirrel repeated, winking as she pulled papers out of a file from her impeccably tidy desk.

Sammi scented the air casually to get a read on the woman. Was she the butt of some interoffice joke? She looked around, but no one was paying attention anymore.

Sniff.

Tammy was definitely serious about this. But what could she mean by *harder cock*? Truth was Sammi hadn't seen any kind of cock, hard or soft, for months, but she was sure that wasn't common gossip. Or was it?

Sheesh.

Was no aspect of her life sacred?

Pop.

There went another lock of hair. Her spiky tresses were always sticking up whenever her emotions ran high. No doubt that specific lock was already pointing at the ceiling.

It was why she tried to keep it relatively short, though medium length was her usual speed.

"So, a harder cock spelled *H-A-R-D-E-R C-O-C*, is the response to just like a plain old COC, or *Complaints on Campus* form, but a little more detailed. *HARDER* stands for the *Habitable Accords & Resolutions Document En Response*, which will spell out the terms of the two cadets' agreed to behavior, so that they may continue their time at FUCN'A, and graduate without interruption."

"Oh," Sammi said, closing her mouth.

There were always plenty of laughs on campus. It was all the acronyms at FUCN'A, but she'd never heard of this one.

"Okay, then. Yes, I want a HARDER COC. Please and thank you."

Just then, a loud rumbling sound started from the front of the office. The noise had everyone's head turning toward the origin, including Sammi's own spiky head. The owner of said growling was staring at her with the biggest pair of deep brown eyes she'd ever seen.

Sniff.

Holy cow! Or should she say bull?

Deeper sniff.

Definitely bull.

Yowza.

The hulking male had her inner hedgie chittering like mad. She felt more thick strands of her hair pop up in every direction. The man was hotter than hot. Shoulders so wide he had to turn sideways to get in the door. Pecs so large the buttons on his soft blue flannel seemed ready to pop. Then there were his jeans.

Whoa.

She'd never known a man to fill out a pair of Levi's quite like that. Made her wonder whether he wore a zipper or button fly.

Better check that out, she thought, and her cheeks flamed. She bit her lip, eyes meeting his intense gaze boldly. She'd never felt such an intense attraction to a stranger before.

But something about him had her hedgie panting and her girly bits throbbing with need. Why had she chosen today to wear her most unflattering pair of cargo pants?

Probably because it went with her equally hideous burnt-orange blazer.

Sigh.

Fashion was so not her friend. Never was. Being the same height as most adolescents did not help when trying to shop for business attire, and since she'd gotten this gig a little late in the summer, Sammi had no choice but to peruse the back-to-school leftovers for appropriate clothing.

It wasn't a big concern of hers until now. She was there to work. Even if it was boring as hell.

Deciding to ignore the gorgeous stranger, Sammi ambled back to her desk with one hand wrapped around her HARDER COC. She paid no attention to the two counselors she'd inadvertently bumped into while trying to maintain her cool.

The crash that sounded after one of them went flying into his desk was hardly noteworthy. Nor was the scowl the other wore as he muttered and tried to mop up the remnants of his lukewarm coffee across his rather colorful plaid button-down shirt.

Sniff.

She just minded her own business. Chalking up the stranger's appeal to just one of those things. And she absolutely refused to acknowledge the whispers that the *wedgie hedgie* had struck again as she retook her seat across from Randee. She would not give in to the mortification that threatened to overwhelm her.

So what if she was a little accident-prone? The deliciously handsome stranger could just shove off, far as she was concerned.

"Okay, Randee, take this HARDER COC and fill it out," she said after closing her eyes for a moment to collect herself.

Only, once she reopened them, the chair formerly occupying the raccoon shifter was empty. Darn it. Where had that little cadet run off to? Sammi was about to alert the office manager when a curiously pleasant, rough-sounding voice reached her ears.

"Excuse me?"

The unfamiliar tones were rich and distinctive. She turned her head and swallowed her gasp.

"Miss?"

Yep. That voice was perfect for the ruggedly handsome face that voice belonged to. It was him. Her growly bull.

Sniff. Yes. Mine.

"Um, sorry," she murmured, running her hands over her hair as nonchalantly as possible. "Can I help you?"

"What was it you said you were holding there?"

"Uh, just forms." She licked her lips nervously, watching as his chocolate-brown eyes followed the movement.

"What kind of forms?"

"HARDER COCs," she squeaked.

13

"I see," the bull said, but managed a straight face somehow. "Do you handle all the *harder cocks* around here?"

"Uh, no." She shook her head. "We each get our fair share."

Somehow her voice had gotten stronger, bolder, as she continued the thinly veiled banter. Who was this mystery man? He sounded American. His accent was definitely more New York than Newfoundland, but she could not be sure. All she knew was she liked it.

"I see," he said. "My name is Sergio Gravino. I was wondering if you could help me, Miss, uh...?"

"Andrews," she answered, unconsciously leaned forward in her seat, closer to the big, sexy male.

There was just something about all six-and-a-half feet of him that made her inner hedgie sigh and tremble with anticipation. He frowned at her, and even that was charming.

Sammi had never gone for the outdoorsy type, but the stranger standing there in his jeans and flannel button-down called to her like no other. She even liked his construction boots, and that was a definite first.

He smelled like freshly mowed grass, the kind her hedgie loved to roll around in. Like on warm sunny days when all she wanted was to sit around eating ice cream in a kiddie pool in the yard.

She never was much for big outings. It was the simpler things in life that appealed to her hedgie's heart. Made her wonder if he felt the same.

"Andrews? *Samantha Andrews*?" he asked.

"Uh-huh, but I like Sammi better," she said, completely hypnotized by that ridiculously appetizing scent.

It seemed to waft off him in delicious little bursts that had her hedgehog squealing in excitement. The silly creature wanted to take a nibble.

Mm, one small nip to catch his scent and flavor. Maybe even anoint herself with that delicious fragrance.

Yeah, good idea.

She could dribble a little bit of it on her back, coat her spines and tail, use it to tell the whole shifter world that she had dibs on the big, grumbly man.

Sniff. Yum.

Snuffle. Yes.

Mine.

Definitely mine.

"Samantha Andrews?" he repeated, and she had to wonder if he was a bit dim.

So what if he was? That was okay. She could date dim.

Do bulls naturally have big brains? They have other big things, for sure, she thought, giving him the once-over.

As for smarts, who knew? Either way, she found herself nodding excitedly. If his mind proved too dull for conversation, she was certain she could find other talented sections of his anatomy to entertain them both.

Didn't bulls like salt licks? Maybe she could set up a round of tequila shots for them at her place. Rub a little lime, sprinkle a little salt in strategic places, and lick away!

Oh, yeah. Mama likey that idea.

The intense brown of his eyes seemed to deepen in the fluorescent glow of the overhead lights. Small, brilliant flecks of gold, like the sparkly sugar crystals that dusted the tops of the fudge brownies she adored from the diner in town, shone brightly at her.

Appetizing, for sure. He was positively mouth-watering. Sammi couldn't believe this was happening to her.

Who'd have thunk it? She'd just met her mate at a job she wasn't even supposed to have and had decided was absolutely not for her. Maybe love really was fated, and this, her being there, was kismet.

Sigh.

She would have to send Sofia a thank-you basket. Maybe a package of Maude's meatless meatballs later that week. After all, she needed time to get to know the big, gorgeous bull in front of her.

"Miss Andrews..." He repeated her name, and she leaned in closer, nodding her head.

Sammi could listen to the soothing, rumbling sound of his voice forever. With any luck, she would get to do just that.

First a little dinner then a little dessert. She lowered her lids to half-mast, peeking up at him through her dark lashes.

It was her trademark look. One that had earned Sammi her very first kiss. He was interested. She could tell by the way he stared back. What did he say his name was?

Oh right, Sergio Gravino. Italian. Nice. She watched him

inhale a deep breath, holding it in for a beat. The bull grumbled low in his throat. He looked down, as if building his nerve. Sammi tipped her head back, hands hanging off her desk as she leaned forward and closed her eyes.

This is really happening, she thought. *He is so going to kiss me.*

The feel of cold steel on her wrists and the sounds of cuffs clicking shut alerted her to the fact that something was very wrong in paradise.

And if that didn't wake her up, his next sentence sure as fuck did.

"Samantha Andrews, you're under arrest."

14

"I don't care if you are a *DIC*!" Alyce Cooper tried for calm, but the llama shifter was clearly furious.

Sergio bristled but remained silent, pointedly ignoring the wolf sitting in the back of the room.

The door to Alyce's office flung open, banging against the wall and echoing in the small room. Her rather harried-looking assistant came rushing in with a cell phone firmly in her hand.

"Ms. Cooper! *Critter Control* says they captured eight stray cats, relocated six chipmunks, and found over a dozen underground tunnels on the east side of campus. They wanted you to know this is evidence of a *spermophile* infestation, but this level of extreme tunneling is highly unusual." The woman spoke at speeds the likes of which Sergio had not heard since the last time he was around his aunt and grandmother.

The two females had wonderful debates and gossip sessions at the large wooden farm table in the infamous farmhouse kitchen, where all the cooking was done for the Gravino herd. From canning plum tomatoes for future use in Sunday sauce, *his favorite*, to baking pies and cakes. The Gravinos sure loved their food.

"Ms. Cogdill..." The director attempted to interrupt.

Unfortunately, her assistant was oblivious, looking at her phone rather than her employer while she went on and on about the pest situation on campus.

"They recommend putting 'keep off' signs on several grassy knolls as they are extremely unstable because of the spermophile infestation. They want to know how humane you want to be in extraction?" The assistant stopped speaking, but her eyes were still glued to her phone.

Definitely why she wasn't picking up on the clues her boss was giving her. At the moment, Alyce Cooper looked ready to blow. And not in a fun way.

Yikes.

As it was, he had his doubts the woman's phone was going to make it much longer. Sergio hated the things himself. Made folks less attentive. Dangerous, especially for a shifter who relied on supernaturally enhanced observational skills to gauge his or her surroundings.

"Eliza! Not now," the no-nonsense black llama shifter growled at her assistant between gritted teeth.

Alyce Cooper was known as a real force to be reckoned with. As an agent, she had a reputation for being a serious badass, and as the director of the Academy, she was not someone to be fucked with. Or was it FUC'd? Either way, that was one llama Sergio intended to give a wide berth.

"Oh, sorry, ma'am," Ms. Cogdill said, almost backing out of the room before her cell phone beeped once more, "Um, what should I tell them about the knoll?"

"Tell them to put up signs for the cadets to keep off the grass until we get it worked out. Now, no more interruptions until I am finished with this PRIC."

"Yes, ma'am." Ms. Cogdill nodded, eyes back on the tiny screen.

She should really consider blue light glasses. The kind that protected against too much screen time. His attention returned to the llama, who cleared her throat and rolled her shoulders.

"You know, I recently started a meditative breathing program you may want to look into," he offered. "It's called BOB. That's short for *Breathe on Bruthah*. A friend from Jersey started an app a few years back, but I only began courses a few weeks ago. So far, so good."

"That is very interesting, thanks. But back to business," Ms. Cooper said, straightening her spine and refocusing her laser-like gaze on Sergio. "There are proper protocols for these things. Coming here under the guise of visiting your peer and co-worker was clever, but then you arrested one of our own in plain sight, blowing your cover."

"The better question for me, ma'am, is why in a campus full of FUCs did no one spot the discrepancy in the paperwork surrounding the suspect? Why was I the first to notice it and her?"

As much as it pained him to think the gorgeous little female was a criminal, all evidence pointed to it being true. Sergio had barely kept his bull in check during the arrest. His animal was furious with his human half.

Sad moo.

"Mister, uh, *Gravino*, is it?"

"Hey, wait a second! Gravino?" a male voice interrupted the director, and Sergio snorted.

He'd been wondering when the wolf was going to speak up.

Grrr.

Here it comes, he thought.

His surname never failed to bring out snide remarks and accusatory glances. After all, how could one of the biggest mob families in the New York-New Jersey area have a detective in their ranks?

Sigh.

Everett Johnson of the Lone Wolf Agency had been quietly sitting at the back of the office, but Sergio had noted the other male upon entry. He did not change places, merely spoke up from his position lounging in one of the plush chairs in the back.

"Gravino? Gravino? I got it," the man remarked, snapping his fingers. "Ain't that the name of the biggest mobster herd on the East Coast down there in the States?"

Something about the way the wolf shifter said his name caused Sergio's hackles to rise. As if he were purposely baiting the bull. There was a time when Sergio would have run toward a fight, horns lowered and at the ready. But he was not a mere detective anymore.

Sergio was a DIC.

Being in charge meant he was there representing his organization, and even Mrs. Leeds herself. More importantly, Sergio was there to serve the shifters under his jurisdiction. Those victims of this identity thief who had so unscrupulously used their personal information, trading on their good names for funds they were neither entitled to, nor had any intention of repaying.

They deserved to have their credit histories cleared and restored ASAP, and it was his job to do so. He would find those responsible and bring them to justice.

Even if they turned out to be adorable hedgehogs that made his bull roar.

Turning his back on the wolf, a dis if ever there was one,

Sergio tried his best to ignore his snide remarks. The man was getting on his nerves, but he refused to show it.

Sure, like many Italian immigrant families on the East Coast, his family had a past. But Gravino Farms was a totally legit operation nowadays. His Grandpa Sal swore he'd ended all criminal behavior the day Sergio was born, and Sergio had confirmed it later when he became a licensed investigator.

"What's he doing here?" Sergio addressed the director, ignoring both the wolf's intent and his hearty chuckle. "Am I under suspicion of some crime?"

"Are you guilty of a crime?" Everett returned, baiting him further.

"Everett is visiting the Academy as a guest instructor. He is here at my request," Director Cooper returned. "Now, why didn't our other resident PRIC tell me you were coming?"

"That was my call, ma'am. I'd only been a DIC for a short while before I arrived here. It was better to keep it quiet."

"And now?"

"Now I am here to run down the connection between the organization known as SCARAB, which Tony Leeds traced here last year, and the identity of the thief or thieves I've been hunting for months in the States. I came to investigate one such stolen identity and missing person, that of a US resident named Samantha Andrews."

"As in *our* Samantha Andrews?"

"I believe so, ma'am. *My* Samantha Andrews, the legitimate one, left the country eighteen months ago with her grandmother and was slated to start her training here at FUCN'A. Your records indicate she has done that, but *no one* back home has seen or heard from her or her grandmother since the move. So, I ask you, how can she be here and nowhere else? Not on social media, not in contact with her friends. It's pretty clear to me..."

"Mr. Gravino, I assure you our cadets are thoroughly vetted before they are accepted. Looking at her file here, there is still no reason to believe our Ms. Andrews is guilty of anything other than being a terrible student." She mumbled the last part.

"But that's the thing, ma'am. She isn't Ms. Andrews. The real Ms. Andrews is a US citizen who's been missing for over a year, and all our evidence has led me straight to your door."

"Wait, a second. Are you saying that walking disaster is a career criminal infiltrating the Academy for some evil scientist?" Everett barked a laugh.

"Why is that funny?" Sergio asked in all seriousness.

The wolf shifter took a deep breath, but it was no good. He just started chuckling all over again, and to Sergio's shock, Alyce Cooper joined him.

"I am sorry, but I don't follow. What is so amusing? There is evidence that this female who was working for *you* is at the heart of a terrible criminal organization that is responsible for the kidnapping of Julietta DiCarlo and for stealing the identities of over half a dozen shifters in the last couple of months alone. Why are you two acting like this is a joke?"

Sergio was having one hell of a time keeping his bull calm. The beast snorted when he'd finished his tirade. But what could he do?

"Sorry, man, but I guess you haven't heard about our little *wedgie hedgie*?"

"What?" Sergio replied calmly.

"Tell him," Alyce said, wiping her eyes.

"You see, it's like this. There is no way Sammi Andrews is any kind of mastermind."

"Are you saying she is too stupid?" For some reason the insinuation bothered Sergio.

He did not appreciate anyone calling the beautiful female anything but brilliant. He was certain she was getting a bad rap. What the heck was a "wedgie hedgie" anyway?

"Not at all. She's smart as a whip," the wolf conceded, and Sergio's bull was placated for the moment. "But the girl has a reputation among the instructors here."

"I see. Has she been victimizing other cadets by pulling their underwear or something?"

"What? No! You see, she gets all the instructors' panties in a bunch when she enters a class. She is sort of accident-prone. *Wedgie hedgie.* Get it? Anyway, that little hedgehog tends to be a bit dangerous in the field. Disaster strikes whenever she is involved." Everett was grinning like mad, but Sergio failed to see the humor.

"Take it from me, Mr. Gravino. You do not want Sammi Andrews in your custody." Director Cooper nodded.

"Why not?" Sergio was so not amused by either of the two FUCs in the room.

"Because you could be her next victim, friend."

"It is my belief she is guilty of at the least identity theft and, at worst, criminal conspiracy to commit kidnapping, acts of terror, and possible attempted homicide."

"Fine," Everett said. "You want her? Take her. A bit of friendly advice, though? I suggest you start wearing loose boxers."

"Everett..." Ms. Cooper warned.

"What? Let him have her, Alyce. What can we do? We warned the guy."

The discussion, and Sergio used that term loosely, lasted

a few more minutes. In the end, it was decided that as Detective in Charge of the joint task force investigating SCARAB and hunting for the serial identity thief in possible corroboration with the nefarious group, Sergio would keep the female calling herself Samantha Andrews in his custody.

He left the office without ever really hearing a word. How could he possibly concentrate when *she* was in his custody?

The collar of his shirt seemed to grow tighter as he tried to regain control over himself in the air-conditioned hallway. All his focus was on little Red—the woman who provoked him like a matador's flag.

That's what he'd started calling the female from the moment he'd set eyes on her. What a shock that had been! It was like every fantasy he'd ever had about his perfect woman suddenly made real.

It didn't matter what the magazines or Hollywood said. Sergio had always imagined himself with someone soft and curvy. Downright dainty, in fact. But his dream woman always had an edge. A sharpness that was both lethal and alluring.

How was he supposed to know that sharpness would be realized in her mane of spiky layered hair? Those inky, dark locks were fantastic. A little rock and roll and just a hint of country. Exactly what he wanted in a female.

Imagine his shock when he saw her standing in the middle of the Conflict Resolution & Situation De-escalation office at the university. Sergio's cock had twitched in his pants at the very first glimpse.

The damn thing had almost busted free of its denim confines, but he managed to control himself. Barely.

All this time longing for a mate and there she was, as

plain as the nose on his face. Truth was his bull had started snorting and stomping, demanding he get closer to the scrumptious beauty.

She wore her loose cargo pants low on her waist, and when she moved, a swath of skin peeked out from under the admittedly loud blouse she wore. However oddly, the top did nothing to detract from her bountiful curves.

I could forget the job, grab the girl, make a run for it. With any luck, she'll be dazzled by my spontaneity. Grandpa Sal would encourage me.

His bull expelled a rush of breath, ready to do just that. Then common sense had reared its ugly and fun-sucking head.

Of course, there's also the possibility she will shoot my fool head off. She was trained by FUC and probably works for SCARAB, after all.

15

For some reason, he'd always been attracted to women who actively tried to hide their beauty, refusing to cater to the whims of society. Or ladies who were simply unaware of their appeal and did nothing to dress it up.

He applauded their efforts, truly. But try as she might to shield her glow, she couldn't hide the truth from Sergio. He was a bull who knew what he liked. And he always found the riches beneath the rags.

This particular diamond was rare and precious. In spite of, or maybe even because of, her terrible ensemble, the female positively sparkled. And Sergio was admittedly dazzled by her.

He wondered how her coworkers could stand it. She was just so darn bright. His bull huffed, mesmerized by the heart-shaped face. Greedily, he'd watched her as she walked through the office earlier.

Two fools had tried to block her path, probably in hoping she would notice them, but his sweet would-be-mate pushed them aside. Literally.

Happy moo.

He would've liked rushing them in his fur and moving them himself with his specialty headbutt or his scoop-and-throw maneuver. But she'd beaten him to the punch.

What a girl!

Her beautifully plump top lip was slightly larger than the lower. So adorable. The feature practically begged to be kissed.

I can do that.

Sergio was ready, able, and willing. More than happy to oblige. Everything about her begged him closer. Like that proverbial red flag, she teased and taunted him.

He'd moved slowly, taking one step, then another, in her direction. She'd been talking to another woman about some papers or something.

Wait. What? His bull had snorted. Red had said something about a cock, and his own had grown even harder in response.

It was a wonder he could stand up straight. His bull was on the edge. The beast had snarled and snorted.

There would be no other cocks near her! He wanted to roar the edict like some conquering king to his new domain.

Uh. Okaaaaayyyy.

At first, Sergio had not been aware of the reason why his bull had been halfway to a full-on rage. Whatever that was, he'd seriously needed to calm the fuck down.

Women had often come and gone in his life. He'd had no prospects for his *happily ever after* scenario, but *oofa*, she had changed that in an instant.

A bright and shiny red flag waving in front of his face. His future was right there for the taking.

Grrrr.

Okay, so I am more than a teeny bit enticed.

He was man enough to admit it as he moved through the corridor, thinking back to that first encounter.

His bull had been ready to bust through his skin, and that was not exactly a normal occurrence when he met a female. Yes, the whole situation warranted further evaluation after all.

The female was truly lovely. Her skin a glorious golden hue that told him she spent a lot of time outdoors. A coincidence, since he himself was very fond of being outside.

Her eyes were a mischievous light brown that sparkled when she'd spoken to him. Of course, those same eyes shot into flames when she was angry. As she had been when he'd cuffed her.

Sad moo.

But what could he do? His hands were tied.

Still, his mind replayed the events. Along with her dark, choppy hair and flushed cheeks, the female had a freshly tousled look he was almost jealous of.

He hoped it was merely accidental. Otherwise, he'd have to break the lucky bastard's hands who'd made his little Red look so deliciously rumpled.

Mine.

Okay. Call it fate then, he thought, admitting even if only to himself the woman was his. Criminal or not.

When else had he ever reacted like that? She had to be his mate. When Sergio had reached her desk, he'd closed his eyes and sucked in a deep breath.

Bloody hell. That had been a mistake. Next, he'd almost doubled over from the sheer force of desire that hit him. Red's scent was so indescribably good.

Like a clean, cool, sweet breeze that tickled his hide while he slowly walked through a grassy meadow in the late afternoon sun. Her light brown eyes had dazzled with the way she stared at him through thick lashes.

Her inviting scent had grown even stronger, and yes, he'd even picked up on the fact she was a hedgehog shifter. Unusual, but not unheard of.

Sergio was extremely open-minded about inter-species relationships. Even when the critters involved had such huge size discrepancies. For example, few could match him in sheer pound-for-pound awesomeness. But this pint-sized tidbit was turning his usually formidable Jersey bull into a damn lap dog.

Silly animal was behaving like a poodle. Belly up, tongue lolling to the side, just dying for her to pet him with those tiny, soft-looking hands of hers. Atypical to say the least.

His animal, while having approved of his human side's healthy libido, never really sought out any attention from the opposite sex with whom Sergio had the infrequent dalliance. But thinking back at how Red had licked her lips when he'd walked over to speak to her had his inner animal bellowing like a regular bull during breeding season.

Damn, she brought out the beast in him. He bit his tongue to keep the groan from escaping. Too late. The odd looks he received from the shifters milling about WANC—the Working and Administration Networking Core, FUCN'A's main building—told him he'd been a little too vocal on his trip down memory lane. But what to do now?

Yes, he'd seen the satisfied gleam in her eye, which existed only in females who knew they were driving some poor guy wild. Her plump lips reminded him of ripe cherry tomatoes. Sweet, juicy, and just a touch tart.

Yum. Those were the best kind, in his opinion. The kind he wanted to savor after a long, hard day. He should've given in to temptation and whisked her away from it all, but alas, he was bull-headed to the core.

The moment she'd said her name, all his dreams of tomatoes and long afternoons in grassy meadows had vanished.

Fucking hell.

"Samantha Andrews." He'd repeated it twice, just to be sure. "You're under arrest."

The agony he'd felt was incomparable to any other disappointment he'd ever experienced. The shame! Even after all his grandfather had done to make the family legit, the object of Sergio's newfound affection was a criminal.

Sad moo.

Sergio flashed his identification to the guard outside the door where he'd deposited his prisoner before going to see the director.

"This is a mistake," Red said as soon as he opened the door.

"No mistake, Red. Let's go." He unhooked the cuffs from the bar in the interrogation room on the ground floor of WANC and led her to Tony's car—turned out he did not exactly fit in the Jersey Devil's mate tiny sedan.

Once back at the townhouse, he escorted her out and led her inside. Tony's mouth had dropped, seemingly shocked, when he saw Red in Sergio's custody.

"What is she doing here? In cuffs?"

"Help! This crazy bull has kidnapped me." Red tried to run, but Sergio had a firm grip on her elbow.

"Be back in a sec, Ton."

The man nodded, keeping the rest of his opinions to himself. He dropped the hose he was using to water what looked like a tiny herb garden and went inside his own abode.

Good neighbor, mused Sergio. *Minding his business like that.* He wished his bull would do the same, but the animal was royally pissed.

Snort. Stomp. Grrrrr.

Sergio couldn't catch a break, could he? The first female he'd been honestly attracted to in months, and she was a crook. Go figure.

Grrrr. Mine.

Shit.

Evading the stares of the FUC agents on campus had been easy enough, but he assumed he'd take some flak for it later.

"I am telling you this is a mistake," Red repeated for the tenth time.

"No mistake." He shook his head, ignoring his bull's assertion that the female was his and he was, in fact, mistaken. "You are claiming your name is Samantha Andrews, yes?"

"*Claiming*? No, I am not *claiming* anything, hay-breath," she snarled at him, and he was happy to see she'd changed attitudes from frightened to angry. "That is my name! Who the heck are you? And what the heck is going on?"

"Please sit down."

Saddened by the fact Red was no longer gazing happily at him, Sergio shut the front door and moved to turn on the air conditioning. What he lacked in charm, he made up for in efficiency and dedication to his job.

All evidence pointed to this female being an imposter. If she had any part in the identity theft of one or more shifters, he was going to find out about it.

"Okay, Red, I will explain everything in just a minute."

"You better! Or I'm gonna have your balls hanging from the back of my daddy's truck."

As far as threats went, it was a damn good one. Sergio's eyebrows raised as he glimpsed the now thoroughly annoyed female from her perch on one of the kitchen stools.

Maybe he should take off the handcuffs? He took one step in her direction, and those amber-hued beauties caught his. Then his little Red snarled, mashing her teeth angrily.

Gulp. Better keep them on, he affirmed. But she sure was cute when she was pissed.

Hubba hubba, agreed his bull.

16

"I can't believe this!" Sammi stomped her feet, which was extremely unsatisfying considering she was handcuffed to a stupid chair with a foam kitchen mat beneath it.

Sniff.

Hardly satisfying, despite her nice, hard-soled loafers. She'd panicked when getting dressed that morning, business attire not exactly her forte, but her shoes were comfy.

Generally, the hedgehog shifter preferred yoga pants and cotton tees. Trying for casually comfortable, she'd donned a pair of cargo pants and a semi-hideous blouse her cousin gave her last Christmas. It had worked for the office, but after sitting in the same chair for over an hour, the seams and Velcro flaps from all the extra pockets in her pants were digging into her butt and thighs.

Bloody hell.

"Hello! Anyone here?" she yelled, but she was still alone.

The studly bull had upped and left her alone after she'd refused to speak to him. Just plain rude, in her not-so-humble opinion.

To think she's been attracted to the robotic brute. *Hmmpf.*

She shivered involuntarily. The AC was on full blast, and while it had been nice at first, she was starting to feel the cold. That only reminded her she'd somehow misplaced her blazer. Just another gift the day had brought her.

Ugh. She looked around, but there was nothing she could use as a blanket in the sterile kitchen. She just had to grin and somehow bear it.

"This is just great," she muttered to herself.

To top off the total humiliation of being marched out of her new job in handcuffs, Sammi's blazer had disappeared, and she was stuck in handcuffs waiting for *Mr. Personality* to come back. *The universe obviously is not done messing with me today*, she thought, and sighed. How was she ever going to get through this?

So bored. She sighed. The tall, dark, and annoying detective had un-thoughtfully left her in the ice-cold room with nothing to do. She was freezing her chubby butt off in the stupid townhouse.

"Hello!" she yelled again.

Sniff.

Alone. All alone and accused of nefarious activities. What would her mom and dad say? And Aunt Suzi? The possibility that this could spiral into another one of her aunt's episodes did not bear thinking about.

Embarrassment flooded her, turning her cheeks a bright pink, which though she could not see, she could certainly feel.

But the worst thing of all was the fact her hedgie was convinced the bull was hers. As in *hers*. Her one and only fated mate.

No. We are not going down that road.

Mine.

No.

Sniff.

Her hedgie could be a real PITA when she got in one of her moods. The minutes ticked by, and nothing. No sign of the great detective's return.

Sigh. Uh-oh. Great. Now she had to pee.

"Helllllllllllooooooooooooooooooooo!"

The sounds of footsteps moving closer had her head swiveling around as fast as she could move it. Eyes narrowing at the hulking figure she recognized as the thorn in her side, she quieted her beastie, who let out a happy chitter at his return.

Have some self-respect, she scolded her inner animal.

"Are you injured?" he asked.

"No. I am not injured," she huffed, trying to turn around in the chair but unable to do so because of the cuffs.

"I was only gone for twenty-minutes."

"You left me alone in this freezing room," she pointed out.

"Sorry. Ms. Cooper called. It seems FUC was unaware of some of your criminal activities, but after I filled her in, she did some digging."

"What? Are you insane? This is my career, buddy!"

"Please stop yelling, Red. I can't think when you scream like that."

"You would scream, too, if some lunatic kidnapped you and handcuffed you. Where is Tony? That was his car, wasn't it? And his place with Sofia across the way."

"First off, I am not a lunatic, Red. My name is Sergio Gravino. I'm the DIC in charge of this investigation."

"Yeah, buddy, I know you're a dick. Uncuff me, please, I have to pee."

"Not that kind." He gritted his teeth in a way that was absolutely adorable, but she let him off the hook that easy. "*DIC* is short for Detective in Charge. As in me. I am in charge of the joint task force investigation into several identity thefts involving shifters. One of whom has been missing for the better part of a year." Sergio unlocked her cuffs but refused to let go of her elbow as he walked her to the hall bathroom.

She pretended his warm fingers had no effect as his hold became caressing on her upper arm. Stupid bull. She would not be swayed by his ridiculous sexiness.

Besides, he wasn't exactly whispering sweet nothings. He was accusing her of something. Of what exactly, she was not so sure.

"After you." He gestured inside the tiny bathroom.

"Uh, we can't both go in there."

"I'm not supposed to let you out of my sight," he insisted.

"Too bad. I have to pee, and you are staying out here."

"How do I know you won't try to run?"

"Where am I going to go? The window is too high for me to reach, and my ass would never fit anyway." She shrugged.

Being short and curvy was a cross she'd learned to bear ever since she'd grown boobs. She huffed out a breath and bent down, oblivious to the way his eyes bulged out of his head at the sudden glimpse of cleavage her new position gave him.

"Here," she grunted, pulling off her shoes and handing them to him. "I can't get far without these."

"Fine." He nodded and allowed her to shut the door.

"So," she called out, turning the faucet on low, "who is this missing shifter?"

Urinating while holding a conversation was one of Sammi's many talents. Came from all those camping trips her family used to take when she was a hoglet. Sharing a cabin with her cousins had been fantastic fun, but privacy was not exactly easy to find.

"A young gopher shifter named Samantha Andrews." Sergio's deep baritone sounded through the door perfectly, and she closed her eyes, the better to enjoy the richness of his voice.

The man was just so gorgeous. But she was still wary. He was different from the type of man she was used to. An American, and a PRIC on top of that. The more time she spent with him, the more dangerous it was to her heart.

"Wait, you just said she was a gopher. But I'm a hedgehog shifter."

"Exactly my point, Red. You're an imposter."

That's it, she thought with a menacing growl. *He might be cute enough to send her hedgie in a tailspin with those big, dark calf eyes, but what gives?*

First off, she was not an identity thief. The very idea would send her great-granny, who she was named after, on a vengeful bender against her would-be-mate.

The senior center was aware of Granny's predilection for revenge and had an extra-large supply of pencil toppers, those little neon erasers, to cover her quills when she was angry.

Sammi might be halfway infatuated with the big bull, but she was not mated yet. Maybe she should let her granny have at him?

Grrr.

Sniff.

Second, why was he calling her Red? That was not her name. Also, she wasn't a redhead. Well, except for that time in college when she'd woken up to a mass of bright red streaks in her short, spiked hair.

That was on account of her cousin Lola, who'd always dreamed of being a cosmetologist and experimented on Sammi after they'd polished off two bottles of real Mexican tequila.

Sigh. Good times.

Whatever. Sergio didn't know about that. Not yet. She figured she'd wait for the honeymoon before she sprang any Andrews family insanity on him.

Anyway... The point was *this* was all a big, fat misunderstanding.

"Look, Serge—"

"It's Sergio."

She rolled her eyes, slightly grateful he couldn't see through doors as she fixed her boobs and picked something out of her teeth.

"My name really is Samantha Andrews, but I prefer Sammi."

"You have to stop it with the lies, Red. You are only hurting yourself."

Sigh. The man is thick as a brick. And not in the fun, good times, sex-me-till-I-can't-stand way. Bloody fucking hell.

Sammi closed her eyes and counted to seven. Five seemed too short, and she never had the patience to make it to ten. That was how seven became her lucky number.

One gaze toward the bathroom window told her she was right the first time. There was no way in hell she could shimmy through it. So Sammi did the only thing she could think of.

She screamed.

17

Multiple pairs of footsteps pounded across the courtyard as Sergio knocked on the bathroom door.

His Red was in there, and for some reason, the gorgeous female was screaming her head off. He didn't think; he just reacted. One shove with his shoulder and the door gave way under his might.

Take that! His bull snorted. The beast was ready to pummel any foe who thought to terrorize his mate. Only there wasn't anyone there. Just Red. And she was still hollering like a banshee in some old Irish folktale.

What lungs! Oooh, the possibilities.

He cleared his throat, forcing himself to get his mind out of the gutter. Sexy criminals still got charged with their crimes. They had to pay, just like everyone else. And if she was gone a year or ten, well, he could wait. His bull was that serious about her being the one.

I've never been a patient man, but people can change.

Especially when long-term happiness was involved. Problem solved. Sergio agreed waiting was warranted in this situation. For his Red, he would wait a lifetime.

"What the shit?" Sofia squeaked as she ran into the townhouse. "Sergio! Is that Sammi?"

Tony followed soon after. "Doll, you can't bust in here when he's questioning her. I told you, he has evidence."

The Jersey Devil tried reasoning with his wife, but Sergio could tell by her demeanor that the curly-haired female was not having any of that. She was one angry chinchilla.

Yikes.

"I don't care if he has proof, Tony. Tell him to release her. Now!" she snapped at her mate.

"Sofia! Thank the gods, please help me." Red sniffed adorably and pushed past him to run to the woman's open arms.

Sergio had to admit she was good.

Look at her standing there, big eyes all watery, lips trembling. Hell. She was very sympathetic. Sure as heck appeared all kinds of innocent. But he'd been a PRIC for a long time, and an honest face did not always equal an honest person.

Unfortunately for her.

Doesn't matter. I will wait for her.

His bull lowed mournfully. The silly beast was practically heartbroken. But he was a professional, and he knew shifter law. Best he be the one to bring her in to negotiate her punishment.

"Sergio, what did you do?" Tony's mate snarled at him, and he winced, noting the sudden change in her natural hue to a more crimson pigment.

Gulp.

He'd forgotten that little result of her mating with a Jersey Devil. Figured now would be the time to do as his Grandpa Sal always taught him when confronted by an angry female. Just stand still and try to go unnoticed.

"Easy now, Sammi, let's sit down," Sofia held the still sniffling female close and lead her to the living room.

"It was horrible, Sof. He cuffed me! *In public*, Sof. You know how I hate it when everyone stares at me," she said, and he noticed her hair starting to point and curl upwards. "Everyone in the Conflict Resolution & Situation De-escalation Department saw."

"Don't worry about that now, Sammi. Now, the good news is Tony tells me Sergio is a DIC—"

"Yeah." Red sniffed. "I kind of figured that out for myself."

Ouch. Cheap shot, Red. He kept the thought to himself, but he had to admire her spunk. She had nerve and grit, and every second he spent with her seemed to tease his senses. Sergio wanted to know everything about the sexy little hedgie. But he had to do his job first. He'd get this thing settled, and then he could see where they landed.

Grrr.

"No, uh, Sammi, not that kind of dick." Sofia cleared her throat, and Tony chuckled, but Sergio was used to this crowd's shenanigans and simply took it in stride. "It means *Detective in Charge*. Anyway, he is here with legitimate cause."

"What cause? I never stole anyone's identity, Sof! I mean, why would I intentionally set myself up as me? The wedgie hedgie, for fuck's sake! I don't even want to be me half the time," she cried out loud.

"I don't know who's been fillin' your head with that nonsense, Red." Sergio spoke up, silencing the other three. "I mean, you may not have been born *Samantha Andrews*, but we will get to that in a minute. The important thing here is that you, *whoever you are*, know that there ain't a damn thing wrong with you."

When he finished his speech, the room fell into silence. Entirely too quiet for his liking, but it needed to be said. Tony and Sofia exchanged glances, but Sergio's eyes were locked on Red's. The female gasped, licking her plump upper lip with that tiny pink tongue of hers until she couldn't hold his gaze any longer. Sergio breathed out and pushed off of the wall, walking to the window.

Shit. I should not have said all that.

"Uh, okay. Look, we are gonna let Sergio explain the charges," Sofia continued, and then her stomach grumbled.

"Over dinner," Tony inserted.

"Then, we will all come up with a solution."

Two hours later...

"THOSE WERE the best tofu tacos I have ever had." Sergio sighed and patted his finally full tummy.

The other three shifters stared at him, mouths hanging open. What could he say? He could really pack it away for a vegetarian. He was a bull, not a bird.

"Okaaaayyy," Sofia said. "I mean I am a fan of *MMM*."

"*Mmm*?" He mimicked the sound.

"No, it's *MMM*," Red corrected him.

"Ton, am I missing something here?"

"Yeah man, listen, it's *MMM*."

What the heck? Why were they all *mmm'ing* all over the place?

"Maude's Meatless Meals to go," Sofia explained. "She is the best chef I have ever met. Works at the cafeteria at

WANC. Anyway, she started this little delivery service recently. Been a real hit," the chinchilla said, stuffing another meatless meatball into her mouth.

"I thought you said it was *Tofu Taco Tuesday*," Sergio said to Tony.

"It is, but Maude keeps her meatballs ready for my little doll face whenever she craves them." He winked over at his mate.

"Which is all the time." Sofia sighed.

Sergio grinned and went to snag one of the crispy little delights with his fork, but the woman snarled. Her skin turned red, and before Sergio knew it, Red was standing in front of him.

"Easy now, Sof. He didn't realize those were yours," Red said, smiling widely, trying to placate the crazed pregnant chinchilla.

She motioned for him to drop the meatball with one of her hands hidden behind her back. *So cute. So caring.* Could he help it if his eyes may have lingered on that ripe, round part of her that made his bull want to stand up and moo? No. he could not.

She was a sight even in her strange getup. The tantalizing glimpse of skin in her low-riding pants was almost too much. But he had control. He was a professional, and he would have to solve the case before he worried about bending a certain little hedgie backward with his kisses.

Moooo.

18

"I said, drop the meatball, Detective," Red repeated, and he noticed Sofia was turning a rather alarming shade of crimson.

"Yeah, sorry," he murmured, replacing the fried goody and grabbing another tofu taco instead.

Forty down, and he was still going. He had to admit this Maude knew her tacos. The tofu was so light and balanced, shredded and seasoned to perfection.

Topped with a *cabbage, carrot, onion, tomato, avocado, cilantro, and lime* slaw, it was freaking exceptional. She'd even added tiny little cups of jalapenos for those, like Sergio, who liked a little kick with their tofu.

"Never touch her meatballs," the hedgehog whispered, bringing him back to the present.

He raised his eyebrows, not realizing the seriousness of the situation until Tony went to calm his mate. *Yikes.* Pregnant females were scary AF.

"Oh, you have a little cilantro lime sauce. Hang on," Red said, leaning over with a napkin and touching it to Sergio's lips.

His bull growled deep in his chest, and the female stilled her movements. Up close, she was even prettier. All golden skin and spiky locks, plump pink lips, and one lone beauty mark just below her left ear. Damn, she was a beauty, all right.

"Sergio, why don't you go on and tell us why you suspect Sammi of being your identity thief," Sofia interrupted, and his hedgie moved back abruptly.

Sad moo.

"Look, it's nothing personal, Red," he began to explain.

"So, you are investigating stolen identities and decided because I have the same name as one of your victims, I must be the thief?"

"No. I think you stole her name, Red. I think you took her acceptance letter and decided to have a go at the Academy. She was a top student back home. Honor roll. An athlete. The works. I've seen your record. It just doesn't jive. You gotta admit it's convincing." Tony shrugged and stood up, already clearing the remnants of their massive and delicious takeout from *MMM*.

"Really?" Sofia pinned her mate with a steely glare.

"Uh..." Tony cleared his throat and turned to the counter, "How about some strawberries, doll? I had Maude slice you some with lemon and that fine sugar to dip them in?"

"Really?" the female softened.

Sergio shook his head. The byplay between the couple was entertaining for sure but dizzying as well. Still, he envied them every public display of affection and tender moment.

Soon, his bull offered.

"No, I get it," Red said, crazy brown eyes glued to his face.

"Red, I—"

"It's okay. You have a job to do. So, I think you should do it."

"What?"

"Prove it."

"I don't think you understand—"

"Look, I need you to solve this thing, *guilty or innocent*," she said.

"Sammi, shush!" Sofia looked up.

Grrr.

"No, Sof. He's a detective, and this is his case. It is for the best if he solves it."

"But what if he finds evidence, Sammi?" Sofia whispered, and the chinchilla's eyes glistened with unshed tears that Red's own amber gaze echoed. "Sammi, you don't get it. Shifter prison is bad. Like really bad. I just can't lose you!"

Soon they were sobbing in each other's arms, and Tony was growling at him. He obviously was not amused.

Fuck. Well, neither was Sergio.

He didn't even want to consider his delicate little Red in jail. He could scent her disappointment and sadness. It was laced with a hint of fear, and that aggravated the shit out of his bull.

But what was a PRIC to do? He had a case to solve, and if she was guilty, he would bring her to justice. He had to.

"I can't believe you think Sammi could be involved with something like this."

"But, Sofia, come on. You said so yourself you only met her after she enrolled at the Academy," Tony persisted.

"There is that," Sergio seconded, though doing so caused him to frown. Hard.

He did not like the growing pile of evidence against the woman his bull was intent on mating. Increasingly so.

After the table was cleared and dishes washed and put away, Tony placed a huge bowl of strawberries on the table. The three talked, hatching up plans or schemes to prove her innocence. Sergio could hardly keep up. His mind was racing.

Maybe there was a reason for her to steal someone else's identity. Of course, the bigger issue was, where the hell was the real Samantha Andrews? The female gopher and her grandmother were nowhere to be found.

Crap.

He sincerely hoped his little Red was not capable of murder. What would their children think?

Like we don't have murderers in our family already.

That might be true, but that was years ago. Grandpa Sal was never convicted on any of the charges they'd brought against him. As for Sergio's *Zia* Maria, things did not work out quite that way.

Grandpa Sal's sister was technically his great-aunt, but she was his *Zia* for as long as he could remember hearing tales told of her dastardly deeds. She'd been convicted of breaking county bylaws by improperly disposing of an animal carcass after a witness had seen her tossing various body parts of what was believed to be a stag through the wood chipper back on the farm.

Truth was she had been married to a deer shifter who strayed on over to greener pastures one time too many. Of course, the normals had believed the creature was non-sentient, which was fine with the rest of the family.

No one liked *Zio* Paolo much, anyway. The human authorities couldn't prove the remains belonged to anything but a regular old deer. And Grandpa Sal supported his sister to this day.

Hell, he'd even gone with the older man to visit the

matron in prison. In fact, if Sergio's calculations were correct, the elderly woman was due for parole this year. It would be good to have her home again. No one in the family would object to Red's deeds because what's a little thing like a stolen social security number or fake ID after something like that?

Would they?

Sad moo.

"I have an idea." Red spoke up, silencing everyone at the table and rousing Sergio from his musings. "What if I prove who I am?"

"How can you do that?"

"By helping you solve the case," she said, eyes narrowed and arms crossed under her magnificent bosom.

"You want to what?"

"Help you solve the case."

Sergio looked at Tony. The man's eyebrows had disappeared into his hairline. He glanced at Sofia, who was smiling at the female and wiping her eyes, as if she approved of the nonsensical scheme. Finally, he looked back at Red, who now had her eyes narrowed at him in annoyance.

Shit. What did I do?

He tried to find something positive to say to her when his bull was roaring a big fat no in his brain. Of course, there was no way. She simply could not help him solve this crime. Not when she was the prime suspect.

"Well?"

"Well, what? The answer is no, Red."

"Why? And for the love of all the gods, why do you keep calling me Red?" She tossed her napkin onto the table and stood up angrily.

The flurry of movement brought his attention to all

those deliciously curvy bits he'd been trying so hard not to notice throughout their meal. The blouse had been replaced by a snug little tank top that showed off her ample breasts and indented waist.

Hubba hubba.

Grandpa Sal had schooled him well on the slang used by the average 1940s ace. A cookie like his Red, all full of moxie, was definitely something to flip his wig over.

Sigh. Yeah, Sergio was a sucker for etymology. Had made a sort of hobby out of discovering the origins of words, and the '40s were his favorite. In his humble opinion, his bull had it right the first time he'd glanced at her. Red was a dish.

Hubba hubba, indeed.

His dish, and he wasn't letting anyone else claim what was his. Nor was he walking her straight into the lion's den.

"I won't be responsible for you getting hurt during my mission. Absolutely not."

"I trained as a FUC agent!"

"And you work as a guidance counselor."

Shit.

He realized his mistake the moment the words left his mouth. Every eye in the room landed on him. He should've realized Tony would take his mate's side when the female began to take a chunk out of his hide for his remark.

"I will have you know the ability to react with calm and logic in order to defuse certain altercations before they become something intolerable by all is a skill most law enforcement officers, *even secret shifter ones*, pride themselves on!"

"Sorry. Look, really, Sofia, I meant no disrespect, but I can't let a female civilian—" Sergio tried, but the chinchilla shifter, who had been bitten by the Jersey Devil and now carried some of his DNA inside, was already turning a dangerous shade of crimson.

Uh-oh. I stepped right into that one.

"Come on, doll face. Let's get out of here and leave Sergio to discuss plans with Sammi." Tony stood up and took his mate's hand. "I don't want you getting upset. It's not good for the baby." He grumbled something else into her ear, and the woman was turning red again, but Sergio had a feeling it was for an entirely different reason.

"Okay, but what about Sammi? Are you sure you are okay with him?"

"Yes, I am sure," Red said.

Was it wrong he felt ridiculously pleased that she trusted him to take care of her? He waited a beat for the couple to go before turning to his prisoner, *aka his fated mate.*

Nervous moo.

"First, Red, we are gonna clean up dessert. Then you're gonna talk. And I am warning you now, you are not coming with me to investigate unless you can convince me you have a case. Deal?"

"Deal." She stuck her chin out defiantly, and Sergio bit back his grin.

She was headstrong. Another trait for the plus column in his mind. Sergio simply could not deal with a woman who cowed down to his roughshod ways. That always left him feeling too much like a bully. No pun intended.

It was simply fact. The women in his past tended to be swayed to his way of thinking, with very little action on his part. A simple stare and many of them were ready to allow him to have his way.

Truth be told, it got boring after a while. A problem that

ended most of his infrequent romantic affairs. One of the reasons he was still single.

He almost did not want to admit that this was a real fear of his. His bull was so certain Red was theirs. But what if she cringed or winced under his indomitable stare?

True, she exhibited quite the opposite in their little exchange. Hell, the little spitfire was practically daring him to argue with her.

How unique! Wonderful. Intriguing even. Yes, he very much liked the fact she was telling him to stuff it with her fierce glare and bellicose posture.

I like you, Red, he wanted to say.

Very much.

19

Sammi dried the last plate and placed it right in her own personal PRIC's enormous hands without even glancing. He accepted the dish, as he had the others, with a deep, rumbling grunt.

Sniff.

Heat blossomed in her stomach at the façade of domesticity the two of them presented. Having settled into a rhythm that was both comforting and efficient, Sammi had fallen victim to one of her secret fantasies.

Connubial felicity.

Also known as *wedded bliss.* Sigh. Despite being not in vogue for a modern woman of the world, Sammi secretly harbored a yearning to be espoused. She was surrounded daily by her goal-oriented family as a hoglet and ever since she'd enrolled at the Academy by career-minded FUCs.

And she wanted that, too. Really, she did.

Was it wrong to hope for both? She thought of all the married FUCs she'd seen or had been taught by during her time as a cadet. Those were her real idols. The FUCs who had it all!

Indomitable pairs like Chase and Miranda, Nolan and Clarice, and Mason and Jesse. Sigh.

Was it wrong for her to want what they had? To be part of a crime-fighting duo who shared a love so strong and true it outshined all the rest?

Sigh.

There, in that rented townhouse, Sammi found herself slipping into the impossible and dangerous daydream of what it would be like if she were *happily-mated-after* with the admittedly studly bull far too easily.

Of course, the man didn't seem too enthusiastic over her wanting to help him solve the case. Even though she would be the perfect asset to Sergio's PRIC ambitions.

Not exactly a FUC agent herself but not *not* a FUC agent either. After all, she had passed her courses. *Eventually.*

Sammi's work as a counselor was only temporary. To help her get over her fears of being in the field and maybe cure her unfortunate allergy to danger. The one that seemed to cause chaos wherever she tread.

So, what if she had to repeat a few classes? *Practice makes perfect*. And if she had an aversion to violence, it was just because, as a hedgie, she had limited resources when it came to self-defense.

True, her spines were awesome, but if she went up against say a rhino shifter, what could she do? Other shifters were generally bigger, stronger, and deadlier. However, with a bull by her side, there would be no stopping her.

Mine.

Her hedgie sniffed loudly at the thought of the big, handsome bull. He was simply delicious. A wonderful prospect to be her mate, for sure. She could feel her animal's agreement. The beastie sighed and batted her tiny brown eyes, already half in love with the man.

Slow your roll, she chided the critter. Too fast for all that now. She still needed to keep her defenses up. What if he snored? Hated rap music? Or, gods forbid, refused to admit that reading was the best diversion *evah*!

Don't care. Sniff. Mine.

Oh well. It took her years to feel this way. She supposed it was only right that when she fell, this hedgie fell hard. It couldn't be helped.

This sort of thing, dinner and cleaning up together afterward, on the regular could be kind of nice. Especially with him.

Dangerous thoughts, indeed. Sammi supposed it was typical of her to catch feelings off of daydreams. He probably had no idea what was going through her brain at the moment.

That was another problem. Just because she felt this way did not mean he reciprocated. Darn it. That was a difficult pill to swallow.

But how was she going to broach the possibility that he was her mate until she cleared her name?

Yeah. Not happening.

Sniff. Make it happen.

Sammi somehow bit back her sigh. She was just so happy with him nearby. Content and intrigued all at the same time.

Don't forget horny.

Okay, that was crass, but she couldn't help her overwhelming physical attraction to the big lug. Even more shocking than the urgent desire to kiss him silly was the feeling of safety.

Truth.

Sammi just felt so darn protected near him. For a hedgie with a *not-so-small* aversion to violence, that fact was like the cherry on top of the already *super-tempting sundae* that was Detective Gravino.

"Okay, that's done." She turned around when the last dish had been washed, dried, and put away in the cabinet. "I'd like to see the information you have to date now."

"No way."

"But you said I could help."

"Actually, Red, I never officially agreed."

"Yes, you did."

"Whatever." He rolled his ridiculously large, dark brown eyes. "I don't care. You are still not getting my files."

"Why not?"

"If I show you all my cards, and you're guilty, you'll be able to build your defense case using my own data against me, Red." Sergio shook his head, making the short strands fall every which way. "And that ain't happening."

Was it wrong that she wanted to run her fingers through the sexy tousled locks? There was just something about his look, that constantly windblown hair of his, that made her want to grab it and pull.

In fact, she pictured herself doing just that. Of course, his head was between her thighs when she imagined it.

Oh my.

She could practically feel that long, thick tongue of his. Imagined the rough slide of it across her nether bits. Yes. Please. She wanted to yell, but bit her lip. Of course, her panties didn't fare so well. The damp cotton was a direct result of her scandalous thoughts.

"What's got you tongue-tied, Red?" His deep voice startled her, and she jumped.

Eeek! Sammi closed her eyes and willed those *oh-so-dirty* images to subside.

"Nothing," she murmured.

"So, what do we do now?"

Oh, the possibilities were endless. What wouldn't she do with a man his size? She bet he could take anything she dished out. *All. Night. Long.*

Heck yeah.

Sniff.

"Right, uh..." She bit her lip, leaning into his space just a little bit. "I guess now we talk." She sashayed out of the kitchen, giving a little extra wiggle to her bottom.

It took only a second for his appreciative rumble to reach her ears. Smiling all the way down to the living room area, she took a seat, trying hard not to grin at the man.

"I won't tell you what proof I have, Red. You can wiggle that ass of yours from here to kingdom come," he repeated, following her inside.

"Well fine, then," she continued. "I can respect you for not trusting me—"

"Although I admit if you wiggle that thing for anyone else, I won't be responsible for what happens next."

"Is that so?"

"Yes, ma'am."

"What will you do?"

"I'll be forced to spank you."

Spank me? She waited for the horror she should have felt, but all she managed was to be intrigued. And warm. So very warm.

"I bet your bottom would look fantastic all rosy like your cheeks are right now."

"They are not rosy," she returned primly. "Now about your evidence..."

"I won't share everything, Red, but I will tell you this," he continued. "I looked into your FUC application. The couple you listed as your parents were not registered with any hospital at the time of your supposed birth. There is zero record of you being born other than a birth certificate filed four months after your birthdate."

"There is a perfectly logical explanation," she said, tucking her feet under her legs.

"Oh, really?" he scoffed.

"Yes, really." She made a face at him.

"Fine. Explain."

Sammi tried not to growl as she watched him grab a pen and a legal notebook from his briefcase. The man was all work, but that was okay. She could deal with that, *she hoped*, and with the fact he thought she was a criminal.

Sniff.

"My parents were on an extended tour of Africa when I was born. They were visiting *prickles* in the area. That's what a group of hedgehog shifters is called," she added. "Anyway, they love telling the story of how this indigenous prickle welcomed them to stay deep in the heart of the *Bushveld* near the Limpopo River in northern South Africa."

"*Limpopo*?" he asked as he jotted the name down.

Gosh, he was cute when he concentrated. Developed the slightest little crease between his eyebrows. Sammi was dying to lean over and smooth it with her fingertips, or lips.

Ahem. Back to business. The sooner we clear our name, the sooner we bag the bull. Her hedgie sure had a brilliant knack for laying it all out, didn't she?

Sigh.

"Yes. Limpopo. I was born there under the light of a rare full blood moon. The prickle thought that a great sign. My father was a wreck, but a couple of midwives were able to aid and comfort my mother. She says it was the most magical experience of her life."

"And naturally there is no paperwork, no government records, or proof of all this?" he asked skeptically.

"Naturally." She shrugged. "They were in the wilds of Africa. Any paperwork was dated weeks after my actual birth. Daddy didn't even have a battery left for his camera, but see this?" She lifted the bottom of her shirt to reveal the soft, tanned skin of her belly, but that wasn't what she wanted to show him.

"Is that a tattoo?" He swallowed audibly.

"Yes. These dots are a map of the sky. It's the alignment of the stars as they were the night I was born. The prickle's shaman gave them to me so my parents would be able to tell the exact time I came into the world by their position. It's the Milky Way. See this big one? That's the Pistol Star."

"Looks like little dots to me, Red." He shrugged, but his eyes glittered, and he didn't look away.

"It's more than dots, *Mr. Gravino*. This here is my real birth certificate."

"Mr. Gravino is my grandfather. You could call me *Detective Gravino*, I suppose." He winked. "But I'd rather you call me Sergio, Red."

He stood up and walked over to her. The bull sat on the cushion next to her and leaned over, crowding her against the side of the sofa under the guise of inspecting her tattoo. He was so much bigger than she was; she had to lean her head back to keep looking at him.

He took out his cell phone and snapped a shot of the tattoo. Which also marked lines of latitude and longitude. There were also wavy lines to represent the river and a sphere to mark the placement of the moon.

20

He sat up but didn't move back. The heat radiating off his enormous frame seeped through her clothing onto her skin. Sammi shivered with need, noting the blatant way he stared. Wild horses couldn't have dragged her eyes from his right then.

Nope. His nostrils flared slightly, and she appreciated his straight nose and the five o'clock shadow, which only enhanced his chiseled features. His eyes darkened to a molten brown. *Like lava cake,* she mused. Sammi was so not looking away. Not if her life depended on it.

"Well, Detective?" she asked, needing to do something; otherwise, she was liable to jump him.

"Call me Sergio."

"No." She grinned.

"Why not?"

"I won't call you by your first name, *Detective Gravino*."

"You will, Red." He gave her a wicked grin. "By the time I'm through, you'll be screaming it."

The promise behind his words sent shivers through her body. His grin grew as if he knew exactly what his close proximity and tantalizing words were doing to her. Sammi licked her lips. Just a little bit closer and she'd be kissing him.

But he didn't move in. Didn't brush his sexy-as-hell mouth against hers. Not yet, anyway. The bull was so close she felt vibrations from his body echo against her skin, making the tiny hairs on the back of her neck tingle in anticipation.

Sammi's mouth went dry. But she shook her head, effectively breaking the spell he was weaving around her so easily.

"Confident of that, are you?"

"You bet, Red. Maybe you'll even sing my name."

"Fat chance, *bull boy.*" She snorted. "I can tell you this though. I won't even say it. Not until I prove who I am to you."

"I get it, but you do know I will find the truth? The actual truth," he murmured.

"Good, then this is all moot."

"Don't lie to me, please. Whatever it is, I will try to help." He seemed to mean that, but still, it bothered her that he thought she was not telling the truth. "Just tell me one thing, Red. Do you know where the girl is? Where her grandmother is?"

"What girl?" she asked, rising from the couch.

She needed space, needed air, but he dogged her steps. The man was like a dog with a bone, or was that a bull with a hay straw? Whatever.

All she knew was if she kept breathing in that delicious fragrance that was all him, she would forget all about what she was trying to do there. And that was clear her name then claim her mate.

"Samantha Andrews," he grunted.

"I am Samantha Andrews."

"Stop playing games. I mean the *real* Samantha Andrews, Red," he growled, furrowing his thick eyebrows as he watched her. "You tell me what you know about her, and then you and I can finish our discussion."

"I can't tell you what I don't know. And as for our *discussion*," she said daringly, "I'm not sure I want to finish it with you."

"I just need the truth. I promise I will understand if you needed an ID to get into the Academy, to get your license, whatever. But someone is hurting people now, Red."

"I have never hurt a soul," she growled then grimaced. "Except for a few accidents."

No point in lying to him.

"I am not talking about whatever happened during your training at FUCN'A. Someone is ruining people's credit, destroying their futures, and a young woman was kidnapped."

"I don't have anything to do with that."

"I believe you," he said softly, and the words meant everything to her, until he qualified them. "But I still need to know who you really are."

That was the last straw. She could tell by the way his eyelids were lowered at half-mast that he was as intrigued as she was. Maybe it was time she grabbed the bull by the horns after all.

Sammi licked her lips and pressed herself fully against him, enjoying the way his breath caught and his dark eyes flashed open. The subtle hiss of him sucking in air before his beast sent a rumble vibrating through his chest made her hedgie preen.

She affected the big lug. Good. But before he could react,

she stepped away. Eyes trained on him, she backed out of the room.

"We're not finished," he growled.

"Yes, we are."

Sergio looked ready to burst. He was clenching his jaw so tight she thought his teeth would break. She'd never been much of a Mata Hari, but even Sammi had to admit teasing the bull was fun. The man was simply too tense. He needed to relax, to enjoy life. She could do that for him. Help ease his workload and teach him to see things a little differently.

"Everything is not all black and white, Detective." She shook her head when he moved to follow.

"Excuse me a moment," he grumbled, heading presumably to the washroom.

Looks like she'd gotten under his skin. Good.

Mates were meant to bring each other balance. Despite his belief that she was an imposter, she knew he was it for her. And for the first time in her life, she felt positive she was meant for something other than causing disasters.

Sammi could not be more perfect for him. True, she shied away from danger, feared turning into Aunt Suzi, but other than that, she was generally a fun-loving gal. Just think of all the roaring laughter she could bring into his way-too-orderly life.

Yep, no doubt about it. *He definitely needs me*, she thought, as she perused his neatly stacked notes on the desk in the living room. A little recon was in order.

Hmmm.

Okay, so he was not exactly full of baloney. The bull had some evidence that there was, in fact, an American gopher shifter named Samantha Andrews.

Common enough name, she supposed, but the real kicker was the young woman was gone. Missing as it were.

Uh-oh.

That was troublesome. Sammi's heart squeezed, thinking the other female could be in danger, but she sure as shit did not have anything to do with it.

Even more disturbing was the fact her grandmother was gone too. Who kidnapped grandmas? The older woman had told neighbors of her granddaughter's desire to seek her higher education and potential career with the Furry United Coalition.

But that is where Sammi got confused. If this other Samantha Andrews wanted to come to FUCN'A, where was she? Sammi had certainly never run into anyone with her name, and with her rep, she would have noticed.

She couldn't imagine another cadet would be happy to be mixed up with her. It sorta sucked to be notorious as a troublemaker and disaster-causer.

Sigh.

Oh shit. That's why he asked me where she was. He doesn't just think I stole her identity. That DIC thinks I killed her!

"What are you doing?"

Sammi squeaked, turning around and knocking some of his things to the floor. *Surprisingly light-footed for a man his size*, she thought, and took a moment to collect her breath. Then she turned an accusatory glare on him. "You think I killed her, don't you?"

"I never said that." Sergio raised his hands and approached slowly.

"You asked me where she was. You think I stole this poor girl's identity and then did away with her. I can't believe it!"

"Come on, Red. This is what I do. I hunt criminals and find missing shifters. Dead or alive."

"What? How could you think that of me? Like I just decided to end her life and pick up where she left off? So, what is your theory, big shot? That I came to the one place in the world where I would be surrounded by FUC agents who might eventually be called on to investigate? That's your big proof?"

"Well, technically I'm not a FUC; I'm a PRIC."

"I thought you were a dick!" she snarled.

"I am the *Detective in Charge*, but somehow, Red, I don't think you meant it that way."

"You know what?" She sniffed but failed to pick up any emotions the bull might be feeling. "I think we need to start investigating, first thing in the morning. You better be ready, buster."

Samantha rarely got spitting mad, but he'd managed to push her that far. And her hedgie was more than ready to spit.

Heck yeah, I am. A big, fat loogie too!

Right on his big fat head!

Grrr.

21

Not kissing Red last night after she'd pressed herself against him was just about the most difficult thing Sergio had ever done. *BOB*, his meditative breathing course, was doing fuck-all for his current situation.

Frustrated moo.

His little would-be-mate was vexing as hell and gorgeous to boot. The scent of her sweet arousal was ambrosia. Addictive, alluring, appetizing, and he wanted more of it dammit.

Grrr.

The line between detective and suspect was grossly blurred at this point in the game. His feelings about the tiny female were altogether too possessive. Too personal for a DIC.

He should call it in. Get Margot Leeds or even Alyce Cooper to put someone else in charge of the investigation. And yet, he couldn't.

More like he wouldn't. His bull was digging his hooves in this time. The beast would not budge. Red was his jurisdiction. Period. End of story.

Mine.

Shit.

He shook his head as he took a turn that brought them back onto campus the next morning. Red sat next to him, pointedly staring out the window and ignoring all his attempts at conversation.

Not that he could blame her. She'd had no options but to don her rumpled pants from yesterday but forwent the blouse. The tank top she'd worn beneath it showcased every curve and dip of her sweet form. It was not indecent in any way, but dammit, he didn't know how much longer he could hold out with all that honey-gold skin of hers on display.

Frustrated moo.

He questioned her this morning, as he was supposed to. Even if his heart wasn't in it. She probably recognized his attempts at catching her in a lie. Not that he wanted to, but his job demanded he at least try to solve the case.

"For the last time, my given name is Samantha Marie Andrews. I prefer to be called Sammi for short. My parents were on vacation in South Africa visiting a prickle of hedgehog shifters living off the grid when I was born. No hospital records exist of my birth." She sighed. "Samuel and Sally Andrews are their names. We have a thing for S's in my family. Anyway"—she sucked in another bored breath—"I wanted to follow in my Aunt Suzi's footsteps, which is why I enrolled at FUCN'A."

"Red, I checked this out already. There is no Suzi Andrews listed in the FUC directory."

"She was undercover for years. Why would there be a record?"

"Look, let's go to the registrar's office. Check out your incoming paperwork," he grunted.

He hated doing this to her, but it was necessary. Once he firmly established her lies, they could work on correcting them, and after she served her sentence, well, maybe then they could have a future.

Yeah, right. You are so gonna be shown the door.

"Watch that Critter Control truck," Red murmured. "We've been having problems on campus with some non-sentient rodents and such."

"I heard about that," Sergio grunted noncommittally.

He swerved to avoid one of the several pest control vehicles that seemed to be on campus that day. Even shifters had to deal with the regular business of day-to-day life. There was no getting around it.

Growing up on the farm had more than taught Sergio that lesson. Didn't make it any less inconvenient.

It was early yet—before regular daytime business hours—and not many people were out and about on campus. Red had assured him the office would still be open for the nocturnal shifters, who would just be finishing their day. *Or night. Whatever.*

He strolled to the registrar's office with Red looking madder than a snake beside him. He couldn't really blame her.

The jig was up. Much like a certain part of him that hadn't been down since he'd laid eyes on her. He cleared his throat and tried to think unsexy thoughts. The early morning sky was still dark, but clear. And that Canadian mountain air was fresh as could be.

This was where being a supernatural creature could get a bit tricky. Whereas it was true, the human sides of dual-natured beings were typically in charge, some traits, habits, and instincts were hard to shake.

"This way." Red led him down a corridor where the administrative offices were located.

He had to admit. The place was spotless. Very well run

and a damn sight better than the human college he'd attended. Everything was shifter-specific and friendly. Imagine having a registrar window open for those active at night. Lucky for them, there was no line at this time.

He checked his phone. It was not even five yet. But all that time on the farm meant he was used to waking early. What a surprise it had been when the little hedgie who'd been driving him mad with desire came knocking on his bedroom door.

For a moment, he'd thought it was one of his dreams coming true. But when he'd opened the door, she was neither naked nor holding a rose between her teeth.

Sad moo.

Instead, she'd thrust a cup of coffee at him and told him to get the lead out. But he wasn't about to lie. He found her bossy side sexy as fuck.

"Can I help you?" The pug-nosed male sitting behind the glass window barely looked up at Sergio.

He glanced at his nametag—Roscoe Jones, cadet in training—and exhaled. Apparently, Roscoe was a student, as well as a temporary employee at the Academy.

"Good morning, Mr. Jones. I'm Detective Gravino. I am investigating a missing person case and need all the paperwork you have on Samantha Andrews."

"And?"

"And maybe you want to get them for me. Now," he growled.

"Sir, I just can't give you files."

"I have been given assurances by Ms. Cooper that the Academy will comply with requests to further enhance my investigation. Are you disobeying orders, cadet?"

"What? Ms. Cooper? Uh, no, sir, of course not." The young man swallowed audibly.

"Well?" Sergio added with one haughty eyebrow raised.

Roscoe practically fell out of his seat and ran to the back room, knocking down several pieces of paper from his desk. Sergio couldn't blame him for hauling ass. Not really, anyway. Grandpa Sal had taught him how to make that face.

The famous Gravino stare had been perfected by the patriarch. It was well known in certain circles to get speedy results. Probably why the old man had such a bad rap among law enforcement.

Sigh.

"You know, you could have just asked him to phone the director. There was no need to bully him with that death-promising stare of yours." Red interrupted his thoughts with a bit of sarcasm he'd not been expecting.

I gotta admit, the more sides of her I see, the more I like.

"And say what? That I'm not capable of leading this investigation? Come on, Red, you know me better than that."

"I don't know you at all." She sniffed delicately. "But I bet you practiced that look in the mirror for ages before you got it right."

Indeed. He had practiced endlessly to get the Gravino stare down. Took years to perfect. But he wasn't admitting that to her.

"Here they are, sir. I copied them for you, so you can just keep them and go." The cadet handed him the paperwork through the slot and promptly slammed it, flipping the sign to Closed.

"Uh..."

"Great. You scared him. Good job, *Mr. D-I-C.*" She snorted.

"Let's sit outside on one of those benches I saw, okay?

We can go over these files while everything else opens up. After you." He gestured for her to precede him.

"I'd rather go home and shower, change my clothes, maybe even have breakfast."

"Sorry, Red, just cause the cuffs are off doesn't mean I can let you go. You are still in my custody."

"What?"

"That's right. You are staying here"—he inhaled—"with me."

His bull snorted happily at his words. The animal wanted her there with him for always, not just the duration of this case. But little Red wasn't aware of that just yet. Soon though.

Mine.

22

Sammi popped a stick of gum into her mouth and turned her back on the way-too-sexy PRIC behind her. His nose was currently buried in the files he'd received from the registrar's office to note her anxiety.

Stay with him? Can it be forever?

Her hedgie was rolled into a ball of anxiety, and she felt the animal's apprehension keenly. After all, Sammi didn't take the whole *living-with-a-man* thing casually.

She was no femme fatale. And this was her mate she was talking about. Not some cutie from a FUC party. And there had not been many of those. After all, who wanted to get it on with the *wedgie hedgie*?

Her reputation preceded her wherever she went. Unfortunately for her. But was it her fault things just sort of went *kablooey* around her?

Sniff. Back to grabbing the bull by the horns.

Spending the night in a separate bedroom had been hell on her nerves. She hardly slept a wink, which was why she'd been ready to go at the butt crack of that haughty bitch, dawn. Sleeping was overrated, anyway.

Okay. So, going to bed under the same roof as a man who was not a relative was strange, to say the least. Even with a few layers of sheetrock separating them, Sammi could still get a teasing whiff of his incredible scent.

She was halfway to hog heaven when he'd walked her to her door, but she'd totally misread the situation. The great DIC did not have tucking her in with a kiss on his brain. Nope. He'd actually come to her chosen bedroom to lock up the place.

There were only two bedrooms in the townhouse. She didn't know how she would have snuck past him, anyway. The fact he'd come equipped with his own alarm system was a little troubling. Even more so when he set the sensors up around her window.

And on the outside too, so she could not even try to disarm them without setting the things off. The last one he placed on her door. That had been tricky, but around four a.m., she'd managed to break the damn thing without sounding it.

It's cute he worries about me.

She might still be misreading things, but wasn't it nice to think he cared? Much better to do that than to dwell on the fact he thought she was a crook.

Sniff.

Still, it had been a long time since she'd had a relationship with a man. Not that this was conventional by any means. On the contrary.

But still, she didn't have her overnight bag or anything. She felt icky wearing the same pants. But how could she waltz into her parents' home and explain what was going on?

Yep. Sammi still lived in her family home with her parents and aunt. She was not embarrassed. Plenty of adults her age did. It was convenient. Not to mention affordable. And they loved her.

Speaking of them, she'd probably better send a text explaining why she wasn't home last night. Sammi was so engrossed in wording the right message to send to her parents after she practically wrestled her phone away from the hardheaded bull that she lost track of her surroundings.

Her text was somewhere between merely evasive and a lie of omission but good enough to get her past her mother's radar. Her hedgie squeaked happily, rereading her cleverly crafted message so intensely so that she did not notice the young cadet sprinting down the path until the petite creature barreled right over her.

"Hey!"

"Oof." Sergio's chest caught the brunt of her fall.

"Get out of my way. I don't have time for this," the young female shifter growled without looking at Sammi, whose mouth was hanging open at her rudeness.

She wore the cadet training uniform and seemed extremely agitated as she picked herself off the ground and hurried in the opposite direction.

Sammi almost forgot the detective who'd caught her before she could hit the cold, hard ground. The warmth coming from Sergio's body was oddly soothing, despite her confusion.

She'd almost forgotten he was right behind her. But the way his large arms held on to her waist securely was more than a reminder. It was a tease.

"Are you okay?" His deep baritone sent shivers down her spine.

"Yeah. I mean wow." She shook her head, stepping out of his embrace and regretting it the second the cool night air chased away his warmth. "A cadet should know better than to run over people. And so rudely. You know, I think I know her too." Sammi sniffed.

"Well, that's not surprising. You only graduated recently, right?"

"Yes. How did you... oh." She shook her head and answered her own question. "The file. You know, you could have just asked me."

"I will ask you when I am ready. Now, before we head back to the townhouse, I thought perhaps you'd like to stop at a convenience store and grab a few things?"

"Sure. But don't you have to see anyone else here?"

"Not right now." He shook his head.

Sammi held the bag with the travel-sized toiletries and one pack of gum as she walked back into the townhouse where she would be spending her foreseeable future. Under guard, apparently. Truth be told, she would much rather spend the time under her guard. Literally.

Sniff.

Unfortunately, she knew off the bat this would not end in any amorous overtones. It couldn't. Not yet. The bull shifter was all business once again as he perused the files he'd gotten from the registrar's office.

"Want a cup of tea?" she asked, looking for something to do.

"That would be nice." He nodded but did not look up from his paperwork.

Sammi huffed a breath and left him to it, heading for the kitchen. She smiled when she walked in to find a covered plate full of homemade cookies and a pair of lounge pjs with a note from Sofia.

Thought you would be more comfortable in these. Enjoy the snacks and call me later.

-Sofia

Lemon drop cookies were her favorite, and Sofia made the best. Sammi set the kettle to boil and took two mugs out of the cupboard while searching for some tea to complement the treat.

"Perfect." She smiled as she withdrew two bags of herbal tea guaranteed to settle her hedgie's anxiety.

Speaking of which. She ran a hand through her soft locks, grateful they'd stopped at the store. It took bottles of conditioner to keep her hair tame, and even then, it was hit or miss when her animal was agitated.

Between yesterday and today, she was exhausted. Really, the entire week was kind of a lot. She'd started a new job, met the man of her dreams, gotten arrested, and was now being investigated for a crime she sure as shit didn't commit.

But she had to stick it out. It was the only way to see if the bull was truly her *fated mate,* as she suspected.

Why else is my hedgie doing somersaults whenever I am near him?

Grabbing the outfit, she went into the bathroom and changed clothes. She could so pull this off as a casual lounge look. Anything was better than those cargo pants.

Sammi put on the soft cotton pants and shirt before going back to grab the tea and cookies. She found a cute little tray in the cupboard and loaded it up with the goodies, heading back into the room where Sergio was busy trying to convict her of a crime.

Sigh.

23

The irony was not lost on her.

"This doesn't make sense," he grumbled as she placed his tea and a few cookies on the desk where he had various papers spread out.

"What doesn't make sense?"

"Look at this." He pointed to the documents in his hand. "Red, I need you to try and explain all this. How can there be only one cadet file with *your name* if you are not the identity thief?"

"I don't know. If she applied to FUCN'A, there should be two," she whispered, lips trembling. "Clerical error? I mean something is very wrong here."

"According to these documents there is only one cadet—"

"Former cadet. I graduated," she interrupted.

"Named Samantha Andrews at FUCN'A," Sergio continued, undaunted.

"And yet there are two applications," she said, eyes narrowing as she thrust a sheet toward him.

"What?" he asked and grabbed the papers. "You applied for enrollment two years ago?"

"What? I did not."

"This first application is from two years ago. The address here, is this you?"

"Let me see." She leaned over him, trying not to quiver at the way his spicy, masculine musk filled her nostrils. "Yes. That is my parents' house and my signature there."

"Why did you apply two years before attending? Then again, almost a year later, if you were already accepted?"

"I didn't."

"You did."

"Didn't!" she growled, and damn if he didn't think it was just adorable. "I applied then waited a year to attend after my application was accepted because I was helping my Aunt Suzi adjust to being home."

She couldn't help her sudden change in posture. Crap. Whenever she thought of her Aunt Suzi, she tensed. Sammi could not help it. What her aunt had experienced must have been rough. Otherwise, she would not have broken down the way she had.

"Some of the stories I've heard from undercover agents were pretty rough, Red. I am sorry for your aunt," Sergio murmured sympathetically.

"You are so hard to read, Detective," she mused. "One minute you are slapping cuffs on me, and the next you sit there with your big, brooding eyes trained on me and I can practically see the sympathy pouring off of you."

"Yeah, well, you got my sympathy, Red, and more." He licked his lower lip, and her pulse raced in reaction.

"Anyway"—she cleared her throat—"it's not the two entry applications that are off. I mean yes, that is strange, but look at the housing exception form."

"What?"

"Well, you have a housing exception form in that file."

"So?"

"So, I definitely did not fill that out. Even though my family lives close by—so Aunt Suzi will be close to a FUC facility in case she needs their help—all cadets are expected to live on-campus during training. But you can fill out an exception form if you have a reason why you can't live there. I knew an avian cadet who was filing one before they got tapped by ASS."

"What?"

"She was selected for a secret program with the Avian Soaring Security."

"Okay. So, you're saying you never filled out this housing exception form right here?" He held up one of the documents.

"That's right. Plus, that's an e-signature. The form was done online, printed, then added to my file."

Sammi sipped her tea. From her perspective, it seemed fishy as hell. She didn't blame him for suspecting her. After all, it was her name and address listed, but the dates and the housing forms were all wrong.

"I know you don't believe me, but whoever filled out that form… it was not me," she said, shaking her head.

Samantha huffed out the breath she was holding and walked over to him. Leaning over one massive shoulder, she ignored the hum thrumming through her veins at his nearness and began flipping through the dozen sheets that were stapled together.

It was bloody difficult to concentrate. He was just so much to take in at this proximity. He smelled absolutely divine.

Sniff sniff. Mine.

Her hedgie growled, pressing against her skin with her spines, demanding to be let out. But Sammi put a lid on the critter. This was not the time.

I have way too much self-respect to jump on a man who thinks I am a thief!

Liar. Sniff.

Oh, do shut up.

Her hair popped, the thick locks pointing toward the ceiling, but she ignored them. She sucked in a breath, trying her best to take no notice of his warm, steady gaze.

"This young woman requested off-campus housing so she could care for her elderly family member. *For her grandmother.* I don't have a grandmother close by. It's just me, Mom, Dad, and Aunt Suzi. I can bring you there to meet them if you don't believe me."

Sniff.

From this close, she could see flecks of gold in his deep-set eyes. Suddenly, Sammi became very aware of the fact she was alone with him in the rented townhouse. Birds twittered in the now late morning rays, but even they could not drown out the increased pounding of her heart inside her chest.

"This is all very odd, Red. But you— Hey, you changed your clothes," he said, changing the subject and gesturing to her borrowed things.

He brushed his fingertips along the collar of the top, and she shivered in response. The touch was light, platonic, but also familiar. Sergio exhaled, and she shook her head, choosing to ignore the brief contact.

"Uh, yeah," she said inanely, backing up a step to put some distance between them.

That was a mistake. The distance she sought gave him a better vantage point to peruse her from her spiky head to her bare toes. What the heck was she thinking?

Then again, she had to admit It was difficult to think when he was so singularly focused on her. Sammi shivered under that long, hard look he gave her. It made her wonder if the pretty, heather grey loungewear wasn't as cute as she'd initially thought when putting them on.

They were a bit snug around her hips and breasts. But after being stuck in yesterday's unfortunate choice of work clothes, she was ready for anything else.

Her cargo pants and blouse were as uncomfortable as they were unsightly. She'd panicked when Sofia told her to wear something office casual. What the heck did that even mean? To a hedgie who preferred comfort in all things, office casual was a no-go.

Sniff.

The borrowed pants and top were too deliciously soft to resist. She'd practically moaned when the cozy cotton brushed against her skin. It never dawned on her that the outfit was immodest.

But the way he was staring at her right then made Sammi a little self-conscious. She ran a hand over her hair to smooth some spikes that were pointing every which way.

Her hair was her one great regret in life regarding her appearance. The fact was she often looked like she'd just escaped from a windstorm or stuck her finger in an electrical socket.

Sniff. Our spikes are beautiful.

Her hedgehog snarled at her description of her pointed locks, but Sammi ignored the creature. This was too important.

True, she had other things to worry about if she were being critical of herself. Sammi was too short, and her butt was bigger than she'd have liked. She didn't tan as nicely as either of her parents in the summer. And her top lip was bigger than her bottom lip, giving her the appearance of an unfortunate overbite.

But those things she could live with. It was the recently electrocuted look she could do without.

Sniff.

She patted her head nonchalantly. At least, it was behaving somewhat. *For now.* Still the bovine stared. Sammi looked down to make sure nothing was peeking out where it shouldn't have been.

Sofia's pajamas were a soft, clingy cotton blend with buttons down the front. They were also a size smaller than Sammi would've bought for herself.

Nope. Nothing sticking out there, she thought with a relieved sigh.

She wondered what was wrong. Then paused. Sergio was nothing if not determined. Maybe he was thinking of other ways to nail her.

Yes, please.

No, not that kind of nailing, she told her inner hedgie.

The man was a detective, and he thought she was guilty of a crime. Surely, he was just trying to piece together his so-called evidence.

"Uh, is everything okay?" she asked when he continued to stare.

"Where…" His voice cracked, and he cleared his throat. "I mean they aren't yours. Where did you find them?"

"Why, do they look stolen?" She glared at him.

"Uh, no." He blushed. "They're a, um, a little snug."

"Oh, so now I'm fat?"

"What? Fuck no!" he growled. "You're perfect, Red. It's just, in those I can see, well, that is…"

Sammi looked down at herself. Poor Sergio was stumbling over his explanation, but she could see what he meant. A flush crept across her cheeks, but it was too late now.

She had assumed that in the dim light of the living room, she could get away with removing her bra for a few hours at least, thinking she was pretty much covered up. But she was mistaken. The snug fit of the thin top clearly displayed the fact that her body knew its mate was nearby.

Sammi cleared her throat and tugged on the hem of the shirt, but that was silly. The movement did nothing to hide her from his eyes. The hardened nubbins of her nipples were visible through the thin cotton, and Sergio's rapt stare almost brought her to her knees.

Men didn't typically look at her like that. Like they wanted to lick her from head to toe like an ice cream cone. She found she liked it. A lot.

The heck with it, she thought, and dropped her hands. Why should she hide her body's reactions? He was a shifter, like her. He could scent her need. Just like she sensed his. Wait a second?

Sniff. Oh, yes.

He was more than interested. The tangy scent of his arousal wafted over to her. Light and airy it floated in the air, piquing her own curiosity. Her hedgie sniffed and pressed her prickles against her skin. She wanted a taste. To see if his skin was sweet as promised.

Yum.

"Sofia left the clothes for me in the kitchen with the cookies," she whispered, noting the surprised look on his face when he saw the two lemon drop cookies she'd placed on his plate.

"Cookies?"

"On your plate, Mr. Detective." She licked her upper lip.

He was so darn adorable, with that thick, tousled hair of

his and those soul-deep eyes. Sammi knew she was in trouble the first time she spied him. If only he trusted her. Everything would be perfect.

"Thank you," he muttered. "Really. It was very thoughtful of you." He smiled sheepishly and lifted the mug to his lips.

"I hope it's okay. I didn't know how you liked it." She shrugged.

"It's great. Really, thank you." His voice was a little hoarse, and she realized she was not the only one denying her desires.

Sammi blushed, ridiculously pleased that he liked the snack and drink. Silly, but true. She shook her head and placed her full mug on the tray. Needing space to think, she carried it back to the kitchen.

Washing and drying the cup and saucer, she turned to see Sergio leaning against the wall just watching her with his soulful brown eyes.

"I wanted to apologize about all this."

"I understand. You have a job to do," she said, making excuses.

"I know, but you see, Red, I think there is something else we need to discuss."

"Like what?"

"Like the fact I have been dying to do this since I saw you." He stepped into her space and dropped his head, stealing a kiss before she had a chance to think, let alone react.

The brief contact was not nearly enough. Before she could stop herself, Sammi grabbed him around the neck and plastered her body to his.

"Same," she whispered before capturing his mouth with hers.

Sergio growled against her lips, and she moaned softly, loving the slide of his tongue along hers. She traced the inside of his mouth, memorizing him inch by inch, stroke by stroke.

He tasted like crisp spring mornings and sultry summer nights. The kind of man she could keep on kissing for hours on end. But if she gave in to her need for him now, she would not stop until she was bound to him.

"You're killin' me, Red," he growled when she slowed the kiss. "Want you."

"I want you too. But you still think I did it, don't you?"

"Red..." He pressed his forehead to hers, and for a moment, she closed her eyes and allowed him to hold her. "It doesn't matter. Not when we're like this."

"It does matter." She shook her head.

"Either way, you are it for me, Red."

"There is no either way for me, Detective."

"Call me Sergio, Red, come on."

"No. And I won't kiss you again. Not until I can prove I did not do this."

"But it's more than kisses, Red. You know that."

"I know. It's what makes this so hard." She stepped out of his embrace, missing his warmth.

"Okay," he whispered, letting her go without a fight.

Her hedgehog whined, and she wanted to join in. If he had insisted, if he had kept her in his arms, she would never have been able to resist.

The fact he'd released her should have made her happy. He was being considerate and thoughtful, but dammit, she really did not want to stop kissing her beefy bull.

Sniff. It's better for us this way.

She really hated when her hedgie made sense.

"All right, Red. We'll go to your so-called parents' house." He nodded toward the door. "Soon as you're ready."

"Yeah." She snorted. "I advise you to get ready as well, Detective. My family is unique."

She walked away reluctantly, leaving Sergio alone. It was the hardest damn thing she'd ever done. But if she was going to claim that bull, she needed her name cleared first.

Call it pride, or hardheadedness, but for the first time since this whole crazy thing began, Sammi was pissed. Someone had used her as a scapegoat, and she was going to find out who.

Grrrr.

24

Sergio grunted when Red came outside to his borrowed car. She'd left the snug little outfit she'd borrowed from Sofia and put back on the blouse and cargos.

Sad moo.

He was irritable and grouchy. Partially because he hadn't slept a wink the night before and partially because he was frustrated as hell. Seeing her in the offensive outfit just rubbed him the wrong way.

"What's eating you?" she said as they drove to the address she'd typed into the car's GPS.

"Nothing. Are you sure you want to do this? To drive to this house?"

"You want to meet Mom and Dad, right?"

"What are you going to say when they aren't home, Red? Gonna tell me they're out shopping? On a business trip?"

"Oh, ye of little faith," she said and shook her head.

"Have it your way." He exhaled angrily.

A few minutes later, they exited his borrowed vehicle and climbed up the stone stairs that led to the front door of a large, well-kept home. Those damn pants of hers dipped low in the back, and when she bent to snag the paper, he caught sight of what looked like a little tattoo over her left butt cheek.

Fucking hell.

She was killing him. Damn thing looked like a strawberry too. His favorite.

Grrr.

"Sofia couldn't give you anything else to wear besides that?" he grunted and felt like an ass.

"Sorry, I didn't pack an overnight bag when I left for work yesterday morning. I wasn't exactly aware I was going to be arrested, but next time, call first, and I will see what I can do." She smiled sweetly, but the glint in her eye promised retribution.

"Dammit, Red—"

The door flung open, interrupting whatever the fuck he was about to say. Thank goodness, too. He wasn't sure if he was going to yell, spit, or jump her bones. His bull was pressing for the latter.

Mine.

"Mom! Dad! This is Sergio Gravino." Red introduced Sergio to her parents.

He stood there for a moment, trying to take in the situation. The television was on somewhere inside, blasting the news. An overhead fan was whirling in the background. And someone was yelling something about cats climbing up the trellis.

"They came in through the window last night. I am telling you! Cats! Evil cats! Fanatic felines! Beware the cats!"

"Hush, Suzi, everything is all right," the tiny middle-aged woman called out behind her before she turned and glared at Sergio.

It was pure chaos. And only eleven o'clock in the morning. From the hostile looks on the older couple's faces, who unsurprisingly resembled a certain hedgie that he was admittedly very fond of, Sergio knew he was in the right place.

This was, in fact, her family home and said family was expecting him.

Resigned moo.

The two hedgehogs most certainly belonged to his sweet would-be-mate. The one who was currently shooting *I-told-you-so* daggers at him with her amber-hued peepers.

Shit.

He had a lot to make up for, but hey, if it was any consolation, he'd figured out he had been wrong about her before they set off to meet her parents.

In fact, after getting his contacts in South Africa to do some digging, Sergio discovered the prickle where she, Samantha Marie Andrews, had been born. They still lived in the same general area. Their shaman was, in fact, the very one who'd delivered her. She'd brought his sweet and tempting mate into the world exactly when her birthmark depicted.

Okay, so he might have spent a little extra time studying the pic he'd taken of her tattoo on the sofa before sneaking into her room to get a better angle while she was lying flat.

No harm in triple checking her story, was there?

Of course, seeing her relaxed in sleep had caused him no small amount of pitiful yearning. She looked like an angel asleep with her hair feathered out around her pillow like a dark halo.

Leaving the beautiful female alone in the bedroom had been hell. Especially after glimpsing the smooth skin of her belly in the moonlight that filtered in through the blinds.

But he was no pervert, and he would never dream of doing anything to betray her.

So he'd left, resetting the alarm silently. Back at his temporary desk, he saved the image, enlarged it, then sent a copy to his contacts at NASA, who confirmed the star placement.

Samantha Marie Andrews had indeed been born on February seventh, twenty-six years ago. Younger than him by more than a couple of years, but that was okay. He had reserves of stamina, just waiting to take on this little prickly handful. The very idea was mouth-watering.

Grrr.

First things first. He had to tell her that he knew her story was true. And yes, he acknowledged he was a fucking jerk for assuming she was lying.

But how to tell her? That was the real conundrum. And now that he knew she was not guilty, he also had to protect her. After all, someone seemed out to harm his little hedgie. Fudging the FUCN'A files to make her look guilty and who knows what else.

"Mr. and Mrs. Andrews, it is nice to meet you," Sergio grunted when the smallish woman zeroed in on him with all-too-familiar light brown eyes.

"This the man who accused you of being a thief and a liar, sweetheart?" Mrs. Andrews asked in a sweet, singsong voice that belied her genuine feelings. Another familial trait he recognized.

Bloody hell.

Anyone with eyes could see she was ready to cut off a part of Sergio's anatomy that he would much rather keep attached. One that, if truly threatened, he would have to remind her would be the cause of any future grandchildren. Somehow, he did not think that would be enough to persuade her not to act out against the male who had sullied her child's name.

Ouch. His bull winced at the imagery.

Shifter mamas could rival any wild beastie when it came to protective instincts. The fact that her mother directed her anger toward him, a male whom she thought was out to get her hoglet, had his bull grunting appreciatively.

Red needed caring for. Of course, he fully intended to be the one to provide said caring from now on.

Mine.

"Yes, Mama." Red smiled sweetly, allowing her parents to embrace her before the three of them turned on him.

"You handcuff my girl, son?" growled her father.

"Sir, I did, but only for a little while." He nodded.

Sergio refused to tell a lie. It was simply not in his chemical makeup to try and con anyone, be they man, woman, or child. He was an honest bull.

"Cats! Was it the cats? They came in through the window last night." A short woman with a few obvious scars came running toward them, crouching by the door but not daring to step foot into the sunlight.

"Suzi, love, no cats came in the house." Mrs. Andrews knelt down and cooed to the woman who Sergio assumed was the mysterious aunt Red had mentioned.

With a little cajoling, the woman went back inside. Sergio would swear she was spying on him from the kitchen, but he couldn't very well say it. Poor Aunt Suzi, seeing her come to this, must have been hard on his sweet Red.

No wonder she took a year to decide about joining the Academy. He was surprised she had even gone through with it. But she was tough, fierce, and proud in her own right.

He was one lucky bull. Or he would be. If she would have him.

"Mr. and Mrs. Andrews—"

"Sammi, are you all right? Let me see your wrists," Sally Andrews, Red's mother, exclaimed, cutting him off.

Shit.

25

This was a really bad first impression. Her parents hated him. And with good reason.

You would, too, assface.

He grunted at his own positive assertion that he would hate anyone who tried to hurt her or even had a bad thought toward the sweet female.

Red was his fated mate. Sergio was not capable of hurting her. The thing was no one else knew that. And what better way to prove himself than to solve the case?

"I am fine, Mama. No bruises. Detective Gravino was a total gentleman. Well, except for the whole falsely accusing me of a crime thing." She smiled at him as she threw him under the bus.

Sweet little vixen. Bloody fucking hell.

He deserved it, though. And he would take it. He was a bull, not a mouse. Speaking of mice, his phone buzzed, and he looked down at an incoming message.

It seemed Julietta DiCarlo had left HOLE. *Against doctor's orders*. And now, Damon Finn was searching for her.

Why the hell the man thought Sergio would have any idea where the mouse fled was beyond him.

A second round of furious buzzing and he saw Director Alyce Cooper was messaging him.

"Excuse me a second," he murmured and read the message while everyone kept yammering away at what was mostly his expense.

Director Cooper's text claimed new evidence had come to her attention that Samantha Andrews was, in fact, an imposter and she wanted him to bring her in.

No, he texted back. *You have the wrong shifter.*

Yesterday you were sure she was your criminal. Now I agree with you, DIC Gravino. I suggest you take the win, the llama replied.

No, ma'am, he texted back furiously. *You have it wrong. Whoever is passing off those forgeries is very talented, but they were not counting on one thing.*

What's that?

Samantha Andrews is my mate. She is being made a scapegoat, and I refuse to allow her to come to any harm.

You have to be kidding me. Look, you have one hour, Detective. Then every FUC I know will be coming for you both.

You can try, ma'am. But I won't need that long to prove she is innocent.

It was pure bravado, but the pressure was on. He needed to prove her innocence sooner, rather than later.

The sound of Samuel Andrews' angry chitter brought his head back up.

"I said your name is Gravino, son? The American mobster family? And you accuse my baby girl of being a crook?" Mr. Andrews growled with all the force of his hedgehog glowing in his eyes, and Sergio had the grace to blush.

"No one in my family was ever convicted of a crime, sir," Sergio explained, cutting off the sound of his own bull's returning growl.

Making her father hate him more was not the point of today's visit. Besides, Sergio should be used to speculation when people first heard his surname. It had even happened at the Academy.

Sigh.

"Actually, sir, ma'am, if you will allow me to explain the real reason I am here today..." Sergio walked inside and took a seat on the couch.

"What are you doing?" Red asked, eyes wide.

"Talking to your parents about the case, Red. I think I should fill them in. Don't you?"

"Okay." She blinked at him. "You fill in Mom and Dad, but I am going to take a quick shower. Aunt Suzi, come upstairs with me." Red took her aunt's hand and led her up the stairs carefully.

Sure, he deserved a little ribbing, but discovering the truth of her birth was not the only thing he'd discovered. Time to lay it all out.

"Well, son?" Mrs. Andrews narrowed her eyes at him, and eleven inches shorter or not, the woman's stare could freeze the toughest man in his tracks. "I suggest you start explaining."

"Yes, ma'am," he said and heard the shower upstairs turn on.

Red had truly abandoned him to her parents for a nice, hot soak. She deserved it, he supposed. And dammit, he would really have loved to join her. But while his current situation was daunting, he figured he owed her one or three.

"I had a text from one of our physicians, Dr. Finn, a

moment ago. He was treating the recently rescued victim of a kidnapping by a known terror threat against shifters."

"What do you mean he was treating? Is the poor thing *gone*?" Mrs. Andrews gasped.

"Oh, no, ma'am. Nothing like that. She simply checked out of the clinic against medical advice. But it was during her rescue that we found documents tying that crime to multiple identity thefts involving shifters that I've been investigating."

"What does this have to do with our girl?"

"This, ma'am"—Sergio flipped his phone to show them the image presently on his screen—"is a picture of Samantha Andrews—"

"It is not!" exclaimed Mr. Andrews.

"Excuse me, please, this is *a* Samantha Andrews. A gopher shifter originally from New Jersey, she'd applied to the Furry United Coalition Newbie Academy a year after your Sammi did. Because of the time Sammi took off before attending, it seems her application somehow got mixed up, intentionally or not, with the other Samantha's. Both applications and information were put into a single file."

"Oh my." Mrs. Andrews covered her mouth. "Maybe that's why she kept getting strange notices all that time. Remember, Sam? The odd bills for housing and such in the mail?"

"Precisely, ma'am," Sergio continued. "But you see, this other Samantha Andrews has not been seen for a very long time. Neither has her grandmother, who was relocating to Canada with her."

"Oh, my!" both husband and wife gasped and held each other's hands.

"Now, I know your Sammi recently applied for a car loan and was denied. What she, and I am assuming you, did not know, was she'd been denied because of an outstanding status on payments to a rather large loan I do not believe is hers."

"What loan? How much are we talking about here?"

"One hundred seventeen thousand six hundred thirty-two dollars," Sergio replied.

He'd seen that odd number repeatedly in this case, and it was driving him nuts. Why that specific amount?

"This is crazy! She has no reason to get a loan like that. Sammi? Sammi!"

"Yeah, Dad?" Red called from what Sergio assumed was her upstairs bathroom.

"Come on down, sweetheart. Your PRIC has something to tell you."

"In a minute, I just have to get dressed," she answered.

He listened to the sounds of her walking from the bathroom to her bedroom, trying with all his might not to imagine the curvaceous little hedgie in her birthday suit as she got changed.

It was hard, though. Literally.

"Is there something else you want to tell me, son?" Sally Andrews caught his attention, and Sergio blushed once more under her all-knowing maternal stare.

"Well, the thing is, Mrs. Andrews, I haven't discussed it with your daughter yet, but once I do, depending on her response, I will let you know first, ma'am."

"I see." She smiled, elbowing her hubby.

"What?"

"Sam, I think this bull has feelings for our little hoglet," she said in mock-whisper.

"If you think I am gonna sit here and allow this hard-headed bull to waltz in and steal my daughter—"

Before Sergio could protest, the sound of something

shattering and his mate's cut-off scream had all eyes on the ceiling.

"Red!" Sergio roared.

His bull pressed hard against his skin. He could see the beast in his mind's eye, smoke streaming from his snout, as he raced up the stairs to see what was wrong.

Chaos greeted him as he opened the door to her room. Clothes, shoes, and cosmetics were flung this way and that. But there was no sign of Red.

"Sammi? Sammi!" yelled her parents as they came in right behind him, taking in the overturned furniture and shredded clothing on the floor.

There was lipstick smashed against the mirror, and all her photographs were ripped into pieces, separated into piles. Whoever had ransacked Red's room had been there for a while.

The complete demolition of her belongings had been done meticulously and with care even. Sergio raced to the open window. Trying hard to temper his beast's instincts while using his detective's training to help find his mate, he looked outside, but there was nothing there except for a damp towel.

Grrr.

"They got Red, dammit! Here," he growled, tossing his cell to Mr. Andrews. "Call this number and ask for Tony Leeds. Tell him everything that's happened."

"Where are you going?"

"I'm going after the bastards who took her," he snarled.

"If they hurt her..." her mother said, but he didn't need her to finish the statement.

"They won't survive what's coming if they touch one spiky hair on her precious head," he vowed.

"I'm going to enjoy having you for a son-in-law," her mother said, patting his bicep.

Sergio nodded, a sense of pride welling up inside as he hastened toward the door. Aunt Suzi stood at the top of the staircase, blocking his path.

Shit. He did not have time for this, but Red would want him to handle the female with care. Aunt Suzi held a hair in her hand and thrust it out at Sergio.

"A *ccccatttt*. It was a *cccattt*. With black eyes and a gray coat. No one believes me, *bbbuttt*, it was a *ccatt*." She nodded her head.

"A cat?" Sergio repeated, and then realization dawned. "I believe you, Aunt Suzi. You give that hair to PRIC Detective Tony Leeds. He is on his way," Sergio instructed.

There was no time to waste. He had a case to solve, and a mate to find.

Furious moo.

These assholes had done the one thing Grandpa Sal always warned strangers to the farm not to do. They messed with the bull.

Now, they are gonna get the horns.

26

Sammi could not believe this. Thank goodness she was able to shift before her captors thrust her into the small cage. If not, she'd have been stuck hunched over and in the nude!

Asshats!

She chirped and snarled before her hedgie curled into a defensive ball. Her needle-like spikes were sharp and at the ready. If anyone tried to grab her, they were in for a world of hedgie hurt!

Would serve the bastards right. It had all happened so quickly she didn't even get to see her kidnappers.

No sooner had she walked into her room after taking a relaxing, warm shower, eager to don something other than pajamas or cargo pants, than she'd realized something was very wrong.

No longer feeling silky and refreshed from the organic honey-sunflower oil soap her mother specially ordered to keep her skin smooth and her hair tame, Sammi had been too shocked to do more than look for a few seconds.

Her bedroom had been ransacked. Clothes torn up, pictures shredded, and makeup utterly ruined. Her personal space had been violently violated, and she hardly got out a scream before someone came out of the shadows behind the door, clocking her right over the head.

Ouch. Bastards!

For the first time, she was grateful for her thick, spiky locks, which took the brunt of the blow. She would have to remember that when she saw her mother next.

Oh, the years she'd spent wailing over her thick strands of spiky hedgie hair and blaming her mother for not being able to tame them like some of her other friends.

Harriet Henderson, how I envied you.

Not anymore, though. She bet the horse shifter's smooth and silky mane of hair would have done zilch to protect her scalp against whatever it was her assailant had used to knock her out.

Probably that old softball trophy I got even though I never ever hit the ball, she thought with a sigh. Maybe her father was right and participation awards were not exactly good for anyone.

Whatever.

She was not about to argue the pros and cons of such trifles now when her life was on the line. The vehicle slowed, and Sammi tensed.

This was so not good. She only hoped Sergio was able to pick up the trail of whatever car or van she'd been shoved into.

The kidnapper had tossed a tarp over the cage before her shift had completed, yelping at the time, which meant Sammi's quills had done some damage.

Ha! You just got FUC'd!

This is it, she thought with a sniffle. Time for Sammi to embrace her destiny and recall every single thing she'd learned during her time at the Academy. It was her only chance to escape and to find her bull the evidence he needed to capture these imbeciles.

Finally, the van stopped, and someone lifted her cage hastily out of the cargo area, causing her little balled-up self to slam against the bars.

Ouchie.

"Stupid hedgehog," grumbled her captor.

The voice sounded feminine. And what's more, it was familiar. Sammi used her hedgie's sensitive ears to try and pick up more of what the female was yapping about.

The way her cage was rocking, Sammi almost lost her breakfast. Then her kidnapper slammed it onto a table, and Sammi exhaled a breath of relief.

"What is that?" an unfamiliar voice joined in.

"I caught her in her bedroom," kidnapper number one returned.

"No, no, not again. Master is going to be so miffed at you," kidnapper number two whispered.

"Why? It is not my fault there was a cadet with the same name as the alter ego we chose! Now I already got the first one and her grandma out of the way, it's time for this one to go too—"

A door opened somewhere inside the room, and Sammi tried to listen harder. But it was difficult with the teeth chattering and scurrying. She caught the scents of several animals, but it was stale. *Shifters*, she thought, but there was something off about the scents they'd left behind. She picked up fear, anxiety, and *sniff*, something akin to adoration or worship. Very bizarre, considering her situation.

"You? What are you doing here? And where did you get that hideous blazer?"

"Da— I mean, Dr. Ranklinger, sir, I come bearing a gift to help further our cause."

"A gift? Let's see it then, shall we?"

The cloth was ripped off the cage, and Sammi blinked under the glare of the bright white lights. Temporarily blinded, she relied on her other senses to help gauge her surroundings.

Sniff. Ew.

The stench of fear was strongest, but along with the sting of chemicals, mildew, something burning, and *gulp*, blood, Sammi's hedgie was overwhelmed. She shrank back into her defensive mode, only taking a second to peek once her eyes grew accustomed to the brightness. She took a look around.

What the holy horror is this place?

Her kidnappers were quarreling amongst themselves, and their inattention gave her the break she needed to really get a good look. Forcing herself to unroll, she took a gander.

It was a lab! Well, of sorts. She'd only been driving about fifteen minutes, so it was a lot closer than she would have thought.

There were animal cages, but they were currently empty. A stack of what looked like exterminator equipment sat against one wall, and she thought she saw a familiar CC logo on one, but it was too far away to be sure.

There was a hospital bed dead center surrounded by plastic curtains, which were partially opened, enough for her to see the sheets were stained with blood. *Oh my!* The horrors that must have occurred there made her squeak. Even more so when she looked back at the animal pens. Evidence of deep gouges made from teeth and claws on the steel bars and concrete walls told her more than words could.

People—*shifters*—were tortured here. And if Sammi wasn't mistaken, she was next!

Sniff.

"You captured a hedgehog shifter? I don't have time for your games."

The human male was clearly annoyed, but the other one, the shifter female, was not done pleading her case.

"No! This is not just any hedgehog. This is Samantha Andrews," the familiar voice said, and Sammi squinted to see who said voice belonged to.

OMG. Her hedgie unrolled completely, hissing like mad and standing every spine she had on end. She could not believe it.

It was Randee. The raccoon shifter cadet she'd been trying to help resolve things with her roommate the other day over at the conflict resolution center at FUCN'A.

Well, shit. Guess she wasn't cut out to be a counselor after all. She clearly sucked if her first case resorted to kidnapping and working for a criminal enterprise responsible for torturing shifters!

Sniff.

Even more bizarre, the female was wearing Sammi's blazer. In fact, her entire outfit was a replica of the one Sammi wore to work the other day. She'd even chopped and spiked her hair. Though, in Sammi's opinion she could hardly replicate the awesomeness of her own spines.

Okay. Reality break. What is happening here?

The young female was part of a kidnapping ring. But was this the gang Sergio was hunting? The one that stole identities!

She couldn't believe it. A FUC cadet had not only totally *single-white-female'd* her, but she was at the center of a major criminal enterprise.

That bitch!

Her hedgie hissed again. The older male scowled down

at Randee, his face hindered by lab goggles and a surgeon's mask. Then he turned his glare on Sammi.

"Randee, you fool! First, you lose track of all my patients, then you go on one of your bender obsessions. You are going to get us all caught," he yelled.

"What-What do you mean? I thought you would be pleased, Daddy."

"Don't call me that. *I* am Dr. Ranklinger here!"

"Fine, Dad— er, Dr. Ranklinger," she grumbled, sounding more like a teenager with an attitude than a full-grown adult.

"Don't you know anything, Randee? She has been seen all over campus with a PRIC. *Ugh.* This place is compromised. You ruined this entire operation. Now, get rid of her. Where is Harrison? You, come here! We have to pack our things and fast."

"How do I get rid of her?"

"How do you think?" he sneered, *tsking* at the female in a way that had Sammi actually feeling sorry for her.

The cadet turned evil identity thief and kidnapper was obviously looking for a little attention and recognition from her human father figure, or actual father; Sammi was not sure.

"Yes, master?" The younger male she'd heard speaking earlier walked carefully toward the man calling himself Dr. Ranklinger.

His own protective goggles and lab coat, ill-fitting but clearly worn in honor of his boss, had Sammi cringing. The man smelled like a shifter, but something was off. He seemed subservient and not.

But what stood out the most, the thing Sammi would never forget, was the intentional mutilation done to the male's nose.

It had been chopped off and sewn shut in a strange symbol. In fact, the scar left behind resembled a bug.

How odd, she thought.

But that was all the time she had for observation. Randee turned around and was glaring angrily at Sammi. One glance told her the *doctor* had already dismissed her. He'd wandered to the other side of the room and was grabbing files and tossing them at the scared male he'd called Harrison.

Before she knew it, they were both gone—letting in a sliver of sunshine when they opened a door to the outside and left the building entirely—and she was alone with *Randee Ranklinger*.

OMG. What a terrible name! Sammi hissed and spat as the female drew near. What else could she do from inside this stupid contraption? Her situation was hopeless. She was going to perish here, but she wasn't ready, dammit! Not before she could tell her big handsome bull that she was his mate.

"I could kill you right now. Little miss perfect. Great job. Great hair. But no, that would be too easy. I want to feel your life drain from your limp body," Randee snarled, opening the cage in order to make a grab for Sammi.

She liked her hair? Sammi shook her head. No time for that. This was her last chance! Sammi took a moment to gather every ounce of hedgie courage she had. True, she was small, but she wasn't called the *wedgie hedgie* for nothing! Who'd have thought she would ever pray for a disaster?

Sniff.

There was a first time for everything, she reasoned, and pulled herself into a tight ball. Using the sway of the cage as Randee lifted it to unlock the door, Sammi rolled from side to side, dodging Randee's attempts to catch her.

"Ouch!" she yelled, and Sammi hissed triumphantly.

Take that! Her spines, while not deadly, were exceptionally sharp.

"You stupid little rat! Stop squirming! Wait, I'll fix you." Randee slammed the cage shut, grabbing a pair of thick work gloves over by a mess of electrical wires.

The female cackled madly as she pulled on the protective hand gear and came back to the cage. Sammi allowed herself one hysterical giggle when her kidnapper realized she had to remove one glove to open the door.

Idiot.

"I've got you now." Randee smiled, her eyes lit with a mad sort of glee.

Heart pounding, Sammi backed up against the bars, trying her best not to freak the fuck out. Those gloves would make it all too easy for Randee to grab her. Just when she thought it was too late and Sammi said her silent goodbyes to Sergio forever, the door to the lab crashed open.

"Holy cow!" said Randee, mouth hanging open.

And holy cow indeed! Standing there, snorting out white puffs of fury, was the biggest, most beautiful damn bull Sammi had ever seen.

Sergio was magnificent. Two thousand pounds of pure bovine muscle. His animal's eyes glowed an angry gold, and he growled menacingly, stomping the floor and shaking his horned head from side to side.

"Stay right there, or she's a dead hog!"

It took less than a second for Sergio to shift into his human skin. His very naked, very ogle-worthy human skin. Immediately, her hedgie hissed and sniffed. HE was naked! And that crazy raccoon was getting an eye full!

Mine! She wanted to scream, but it seemed like Randee

was more concerned with the idea of finishing her job. Good for her.

"Unhand my mate!" roared Sergio, and Sammi had to admit he was the only person in the world she wanted to hear from at that moment.

Randee squeaked, dropping the cage, and Sammi raced out. Free at last!

Sammi scurried across the floor over wires and tools, toward the sound of her mate's angry roar. She allowed herself a second to feel the joy racing through her at the thought that she'd been saved. Just a few more feet and she was home free. Then maybe later she could claim her bodacious bull.

"It's all over, raccoon. We know your game and who you work for. Put your hands up and I'll read you your rights," he growled.

"Not so fast, beef breath. I still got your female right here," the crazy former cadet chittered and struck.

It was just a few more feet. But before Sammi reached safety, something knocked her sideways and she was being scooped backward by a net that was attached to a long pole. The kind *Critter Control* used.

OMG. That was what the *CC* stood for. She was in a Critter Control facility. Or something designed to look like one.

Struggling to get out of the net, she soon realized the futility. Her spines kept getting caught in the mesh, and all she managed was to get herself tangled.

Sergio growled again, stepping closer to where Randee now held Sammi captive off the floor. She moved the net over the rim of a steel barrel, the contents of which smelled like hell on earth to her hedgie's sensitive nose.

"You take another step toward me and I will drown your precious mate in this vat of toxic chemicals."

"Just had that lying around, did you?" Sergio grunted.

"Always," Randee snickered. "The doctor mixes his own medicines to help solve our problem."

"Whose problem?"

"*Our* problem." She snorted. "Yours, mine, hers. He is a genius, and he will fix everything."

"I hate to break it to you, lady, but my only problem right now is you." He inched closer.

"Ha! That's not true. Look at you. A glorified hamburger. A walking steak. I mean, how can you even live with yourself? You filthy, disgusting—"

That was all Sammi could take of *little miss copycat* talking down to her man. She hissed loudly, clicking her teeth and straightening her spines so that they pinged the pole, causing the female to jerk in surprise. The net swayed precariously, and that was all she needed.

Sammi twisted herself so that she was far away from the chemicals. Switching skins in the blink of an eye so that she was no longer dangling precariously over a vat of toxic waste, she pulled the pole toward her, bringing Randee, who was so shocked she actually tightened her grip on the thing, right along with it.

"Hey, copycat," she snarled, "that's my mate you're talking about!"

Then she socked the little vermin right in the nose. The surprised female yelped then slumped to the ground with a satisfying thud.

"Red!"

Sammi's head whipped around to where Sergio stood, mouth hanging open in surprise. He shook his head and ran to her, holding her tight against him in a hug. One she gladly returned.

What began as joy at being saved and reunited soon turned to something else. Sergio growled as she stepped back and tucked her hair behind her ears, blushing as her big ol' bull got a load of her in her birthday suit.

"You, uh, still got those handcuffs?"

"Not here, but we got these." He held up a pair of extra-strength zip-ties the mad doctor had lying around.

"Wanna use them?"

"You bet, Red." He grinned, moving toward Sammi.

"Not on me, you one-track-minded bovine. On her. Cuff that rodent, before she escapes." She pointed to the female, who was somehow stirring.

Sergio growled and bent down, using a few reinforced steel zip-ties to make cuffs for the female's legs and hands. Once she was secured, he turned back to Sammi, who was only now feeling the chill of the laboratory.

"I love looking at you, Red, but put these on so I don't have to gore anyone for seeing you like that," he grunted, grabbing a pair of scrubs from one of the shelves.

"There're some boxes in here. Looks like illegal documents, passports, and stuff," Sergio grunted and handed her the top.

"Is it related to your case?"

"Could be, but we got time to figure it out. Just glad you're safe, Red."

He grinned and shrugged on the bottoms at her insistence while Sammi pulled the top on over her spiky head just in time for the cavalry to arrive.

"Serg? Yo, *bruthah*, you in there?" Tony Leeds shouted as he ran into the room, a large semi-automatic in his grip.

"Ah. I see the gang's all here. And look, you got me a

present," Tony snarled at the female raccoon, who was squirming against her cuffs.

Tony took custody of the prisoner, while Sergio used his bulk to block Sammi from the Devil's view. It was sweet in a macho-chauvinistic kind of way. But Sammi didn't really mind. After all, she didn't want to be even half-naked for anyone but him at the moment.

"Thanks, Tony."

"You got it. But uh, I had to call the boss, and Grandmother Leeds is a stickler for rules. Like a certain bull I know. Anyway, she called FUC right away and gave them all the details, including that hair Aunt Suzi found. Raccoon hair to be exact."

"Thanks, *bruthah.*" Sergio nodded. "Better get her Mirandized, and into our custody before they take credit. We'll wait for them to arrive," he said.

The Jersey Devil just grinned and waved, frog-marching Randee, who was whimpering and muttering everything from death threats to strange nursery rhymes as he tugged her along.

"Creepy little fucker, isn't she?" Sammi murmured.

"Got that right. What's with her outfit and hair?"

"I dunno. Guess she was trying to imitate me for whatever reason." She ducked her head, shy now with him.

"You okay, Red?" Sergio asked.

His big, muscular chest was so close, so bare. All she wanted was to lean in and take a nice, long lick. She'd been daydreaming about anointing herself with his scent from the moment she saw him. Her pulse raced, and warmth began to spread through her body.

"Yeah, I'm okay, thanks." She bit her lip. "I mean I think so. I guess, uh, that is, well, we should talk about everything," she murmured, walking backward.

Truth was she felt a little unsure now that they had both used the *m*-word toward the other. All they did was kiss, but that didn't matter. Her entire body was on fire with need. Between that and the thunderous pounding of her heart inside her chest, Sammi knew this was right.

"I want that too. I want everything with you."

"You do? Like, really?" She bit her lip and waited, but instead of desire in his deep, brown gaze, she saw horror.

"Red!"

Unfortunately, his warning came a moment too late. Sammi had forgotten all about the vat of toxins sitting precariously in the middle of the room. She'd been trying to accept the fact this was all real. She was meant to be with him. Her one true and fated mate.

But, of course, in true *wedgie hedgie* fashion, she bumped her hip into said barrel. The vat of stinky, toxic waste wobbled and tipped. Just her luck.

Sigh.

The sizzling sounds of toxic chemicals hitting the floor froze her to stone, but she had nothing to fear. Sergio, *her mate*, moved like lightning. The bull had her in his arms and over his shoulder before she knew what was happening.

Her borrowed shirt rode up her stomach as the brawny bovine hauled ass, mainly her large, curvy one, out the door. Speaking of ASS, while hers was on display, a slew of FUC and ASS agents arrived on the scene just in time to see the secret lab explode.

"Holy fuck!" shouted the usually prim and proper Director of the Furry United Coalition Newbie Academy, Alyce Cooper, when the explosion doubled, sending shooting flames and smoke straight up into the sky like a mini A-bomb.

"You can say that again," Everett Johnson of the Lone Wolf Agency said.

He'd been one of Sammi's old instructors, and he stood beside the director with his head back and mouth hanging open at the level of destruction.

"You think there's any evidence left?" Jessie Cygnclair asked her mate, Mason Brownsmith, but the bear shifter shrugged, eyes still staring at the now bright orange and green flames. That would be the toxins, of course.

"Whoa. Hey now. I guess that *hedgie* couldn't have a *wedgie* after all." Everett smirked, catching the attention of her angry bull as he attempted to shield her ass with his hand.

He turned around with Sammi still on his shoulder, snarling at the wolf.

"I would punch you in the face, dog breath, but then I'd have to put down my mate."

"Mate, huh? Okay, bro, chill. My bad," said the wolf, backing up, but still chuckling.

"Take your mate home, Detective Gravino. We will investigate what is left of this facility, and you and I will talk in the morning."

"Yes, ma'am," Sergio grumbled, catching the keys she tossed his way.

Sergio moved her from his shoulder to his arms, princess-style, and slid her into the seat carefully as if she were fine china. Considering he was a bull, that analogy left a lot to be desired. But Sammi was so captivated by his rapt stare and attention she didn't mind one bit.

"Call your parents, Red. Tell them you're safe."

She nodded and took the cell phone he grabbed from the center console and dialed.

"Mom? Dad? No, yeah, I am safe." She covered the

receiver. "They want to know when I am coming home," she whispered, eyes on his handsome face.

He took the phone.

"Hello, Mr. and Mrs. Andrews, this is Sergio Gravino. I just wanted you to know I am taking your daughter home with me. But don't worry about a thing. I plan on making her very happy." There was a pause. "I am, sir. Yes, ma'am. Okay. Yes, sir. And thank you, *er*, *Mom*," he mumbled and blushed, handing Sammi back the phone.

"I'll talk to you later. Love you too," she said and clicked the phone off.

Did she hear him right? Was the big ol' bull ready to do what she thought he was ready to do?

Sammi could hardly wait.

27

Sergio broke all sorts of speed limits driving to his rented townhouse. Tony was sitting on his porch swing with his mate when Sergio hurried by with Red in his arms.

"Hey, Serg, I got the raccoon in PRIC custody," Tony yelled, but Sergio just nodded.

Couldn't talk. Not now.

"Sammi, thank the gods you're safe!"

"Yeah, thank you! Sorry, we're in a rush." Red giggled as he searched for the keys, gave up, then broke the door in.

"The door," she scolded.

"Use the chain, Red," he commanded, and she did, hanging over his shoulder since he still would not put her down.

He carried his precious cargo all the way through the room where he'd slept the night before, passing the bed, and headed into the enormous bathroom.

"Oh wow," she said as he leaned over and turned on the massive six-headed shower.

Finally, Sergio thought as he held her tight before sliding her down his body. To say he'd been in a state of panic ever since he'd seen her towel tossed on the grassy ground would be a gross understatement.

Sergio had been in a total fucking blind fury. Like a bull at the gate. He'd shifted faster than ever before and followed the path the van had taken with his female. Sure, they had a lot to discuss, but right now, he was running on pure instinct.

"Let's get you clean, Red," he muttered, peeling the scratchy blue scrub carefully off her body.

She nodded her head and lifted her arms, helping him undress her. Then her small hands when to his scrubs, but he stopped her.

"If you do that, this will be over far too quickly. Let me take care of you, please, Red. I need to."

Sergio had never begged anyone in his entire life. Not even when he was a kid and Grandpa Sal withheld the first crop of sweet summer corn from the young bull unless he cleaned his room.

But he'd get down on his knees if she wanted him to, just for the privilege of being near her. He sucked in a breath as she lowered her arms, drinking in the natural *Cytherean* beauty of his fated mate.

She lifted her face proudly, and Sergio was undone. There was nothing more beautiful than a confident woman. And *his* confident woman, so comfortable and gorgeous in her honey-gold skin, was a veritable knockout.

Her eyes were still on his while she stepped under the spray of the six separate showerheads. Sergio's cock hardened in the scrubs. Fuck, he regretted not letting her take them off, as the itchy material was like sandpaper against his flesh.

"All right, *Detective*, I'm in." She arched one eyebrow and leaned her head back, allowing the water to cascade through her unruly locks.

How he loved those layered spikes! They were so pert and spunky. Just like her. Wonderful. So caught up in his thoughts, Sergio's mind went to mush as she took some soap and spread it over her curves with her bare hands.

She grinned as she cupped her breasts, rubbing the mounds and teasing the nipples until they were hard and pointed under the glossy sheen of Ivory shower wash.

Sergio growled. His cock twitched. But he could control himself. Until her naughty hands slipped farther down her soft belly, over her hips, and around to the short, cropped curls that tried to hide her sex from him.

"Mine," he growled, stepping into the shower, scrubs, and all.

Red's shocked eyes widened, and her mouth opened as Sergio dropped down to the floor. Not one fuck was given for the scrubs by either of them.

Nope. All his fucks are mine now.

Happy sniff.

The sight of her little fingers parting her pussy was more than he could take. She was his, dammit. And he was going to have her. Now.

Sergio lifted one of her plump, perfect legs over his shoulder and buried his face right into her core. Lost to the sweetness of her honeyed sex, Sergio used his tongue and free hand to work his steamy little Red into a frenzied state.

Bloody hell. She was divine. Sweet ambrosia to his senses, which were now firing away like mad. His heart thudded in his chest, and his bull growled deep inside of him. The rumble vibrated through to his lips, causing his sweet mate to tip over the edge. But he was there to catch her, drinking down every last drop as her orgasm rang through, squeezing his fingers.

"Oh gods," she moaned, pulling on his hair until he was standing up.

"Sergio," he growled, shoving his soaked scrubs down and freeing his thick, engorged cock.

"What?" she said, eyes focused on his dick.

"My name. Say my name," he commanded as he grabbed her by the waist and lifted her up.

Red growled, hugging herself to him tightly and wrapping her legs around his waist.

"Please, need you," she moaned, and he was well aware of her state.

He was hanging on by a thread himself, truth be told. Mating fever was something shifters knew of, but Sergio never really thought about it. Never considered he would be the willing victim of uncontrollable, unimaginable desire. But it was more than sex. These past few days with his Red had told him love could come quickly on the wings of fate.

"Sergio," she moaned and crashed her mouth to his.

Fuck yeah. Sergio deepened the kiss. He thrust his tongue into her mouth, staking his claim there as he intended to on every inch of the delectable little hedgie.

Mine.

He used his thick fingers to spread her lips. She moaned again, sucking on his tongue while he found her clit with his thumb. Sergio teased and pressed on the bud, heightening her pleasure, while stretching her sheath with his fingers.

A two-thousand-pound Jersey bull when shifted, Sergio was no slouch in his human skin either. He was big all over.

Red was so tiny and petite. A curvy handful for sure, but he needed her ready. Would never risk their coming together being anything other than fan-fucking-tastic.

"Now, need you now," Red yelled, and he obeyed, sliding his cock all the way to the hilt.

Holy fuck. Her sex squeezed him so tightly that Sergio almost came with that first thrust. She was so hot, so tight, and so very perfect in every way, shape, and form.

Mine.

Hips thrusting, Sergio grabbed onto the round globes of her perfect ass. Something he was looking forward to exploring later in bed. She shuddered against him. Her arms wound tightly around his thick neck. Thank fuck, he was strong as a bull, cause once his mate started to come for the second time, she tightened her hold.

Growling his pleasure, Sergio continued to stretch her walls, sliding his dick in and out of her plump pussy lips and grasping sheath, oblivious to the shower water turning cold. Over and over again, he slid his cock in and out, riding out her orgasm until the next one started. Sergio simply couldn't get enough.

He wanted to be buried deep inside of her forever. Was that possible? Maybe. Definitely. Fuck yes. He could make a home inside her heated core.

"Sergio!" She screamed his name this time, and he deepened his strokes, grinding his pubis into her clit.

This time he followed her into oblivion, taking each rippling aftershock to further his own pleasure.

Mine, he thought as he slid his mouth over the soft skin between her shoulder and neck and bit down with the sharp edge of his blunted teeth. Sergio was just in time to feel the piercing shock of pain that was over as quickly as it started from her own mating mark, which she placed just over his heart.

From that slight discomfort swelled the most incredible bliss he had ever felt, and Sergio spilled his seed deep inside her womb. White-hot waves of ecstasy swelled like an uncontrollable tide as he came, and came, and came. And fuck yes, she was right there with him.

He turned off the shower and carried her limp body to the bed, snagging two fluffy towels off the shelf and wrapping them around her before falling onto the mattress.

"That was..." She tried to speak, but she was still gasping.

"Yeah," he agreed, struggling for breath himself.

"We never talked." She shook her head, but her eyes were smiling, and it was all the affirmation he needed.

Well, maybe.

"I love you, Red." He smiled. "And we can talk for the next hundred years if you want."

Her face blossomed under his words, and Sergio was struck once more at how incredibly beautiful his mate was. His mate. And she really was that now.

Mine.

"I love you too, Sergio."

"Hey." He grinned, kissing her nose and her lips, taking his time to tease the plump upper one. "You said my name."

"Well"—she shrugged—"we solved the case."

"True. Sort of." He frowned.

"Oh, my gods." She sat up, jostling him to the side. "You're right! Come on, I have an idea on where to find your missing Samantha Andrews!"

"What? Now?"

"Yes, now!"

Sergio didn't ask again. He trusted his mate and her instincts. About time he showed her.

He grabbed some clothes from the dresser and handed her a pair of sweats.

"Sorry, Red, that is all I have."

"No, it's not." She grinned. "Now you have me."

Sergio's Jersey bull snorted proudly at her statement. In fact, he was practically glowing by the time they dressed and went to pick up Tony and Sofia to follow Red's lead.

Funny how he'd started out investigating her and it looked like she'd solved the mystery after all. Not that she was telling him anything yet. Didn't matter. He had his mate, and he could wait till she was ready to spill.

Happy moo.

28

Sammi knelt down and lifted the "keep off the grass" sign Critter Control had placed on one of the grassy knolls on campus.

Following her hunch, she and Sergio, along with Tony and Sofia and a whole team of FUCs, were now in the process of removing the so-called humane traps and treatments CC had left to take care of the rodent problem on campus.

As suspected, the traps contained packets of food, heavily dosed with a toxic mix of chemicals identical to the ones in the lab where Sammi had been brought by her kidnappers.

Alyce Cooper met them there. She had her teams set up floodlights in certain areas so as not to disturb those with supernaturally enhanced night vision. Sammi was not gifted with such, but others were.

"I found something here," Dawn—Everett Johnson's mate—called out from her position on the ground near one of the underground tunnels' entrances.

"Sergio." Sammi waved in his direction, and he came bounding over.

The two jogged to where Dawn sat, cuddling something to her chest. As they neared, she saw it was two tiny critters. Gopher, to be exact.

"Is that...?" Sergio's mouth opened.

His entire expression filled with awe. Big brown eyes went from the gophers to Sammi and back again. Soon, other critters filed out of the tunnel, including a six-foot American alligator that stretched the thing to its max capacity.

"They're shifters"—Everett scratched his head—"but why are they hiding?"

"Because they escaped from the lab and Dr. Ranklinger has been going crazy trying to find them," Sammi murmured, bending down to eye level. "Hi. My name is Samantha Andrews too. A lot of people have been looking for you, and they are anxious to talk to you. But we can wait until you're ready, okay?"

"I don't believe it." Alyce Cooper sidled up to them, shaking her head. ""Codgill! Get me Mrs. Leeds on the line, and someone give Finn a courtesy call. I'm sure he'll want to slither in on these events."

~

A few hours later in a FUC meeting room...

"RED, this is Julietta Di Carlo and Dr. Damon Finn." Sergio introduced her to the female he'd rescued that started this whole thing and the doctor who'd followed her when she left HOLE to find Sergio at FUCN'A.

Poor little mouse looked at her with enormous eyes, and Sammi had the distinct impression Julietta had been crushing on her bull. Eyebrows raised, Sammi let out a long exhale, figuring she could afford to be gracious. Especially since a certain steely-eyed doc was staring daggers at the mouse.

Sniff. Interesting.

The FUC agents familiar with rehabilitating rescued experiments set to work, providing food and water and guiding those who changed back into human form to their accommodations. The academy had a whole dorm section added on for experiments—shifters who needed a place to stay while they figured out how to embark on the next chapter of their lives, and humans-turned-shifters who had to learn how to control their new abilities.

Some agents stayed outside with those who still huddled in their animal shapes, needing time to shift back to their human forms.

"Here you go, Red." Sergio strode toward her with a cup of coffee and, gods bless him, a cheese and cherry Danish.

"Thank you." She smiled. "How did the conversation with Mrs. Spirito go?"

"Very well. Turns out her granddaughter answered a scam letter phishing for easy marks. Told her she was picked to join Her Majesty's special mailing list and offered a scholarship to the school of her dreams in Canada."

"No way!"

"Yes way." Sergio snorted. "And the whole thing with that crazy number, the $117,632 loan we kept seeing? Nothing important. Turns out Randee the raccoon is a little more messed up than we thought on account of her evil scientist father experimenting on her since she was seven."

"Wow! I can't believe it."

"Mrs. Leeds told Tony to give FUC access to her. It was a

good idea. She will finally get the help she needs."

"I am glad, but I am worried about these shifters, Sergio. I mean Ranklinger is crazy. And we lost him."

"It's okay, Red. We will find him. Now, how are you, really?"

Exhaustion was starting to make her droop. Concerned, the beguiling bovine grabbed a chair and, to her confusion, sat down. Then he pulled her close and balanced her gently on his lap and understanding dawned.

Snuggling closer, she held her goodies and sipped the coffee, but that was not enough for her bull. Rubbing her back with one hand, he took the pastry and fed her bite by bite.

"I can't believe we found all these missing shifters," she said when she could not eat another bite.

"You found them, Red. And I can believe it. You are a FUC agent after all."

"Hardly." She sniffed, shaking her head.

"Didn't I tell you? Alyce Cooper wants to see you first thing tomorrow." He grinned widely, dropping a kiss on her cheek.

"What? She wants to see me?"

"Yep. Said she needed you to keep digging into this investigation since Ranklinger got away. Now that we know he is the evil behind the group known as SCARAB, we have to find him."

"But you're a PRIC, Sergio, and if I'm going to be a full-fledged FUC, how can we work together?"

"Aww, come on, Red. Did you forget I'm the detective in charge of this particular joint task force?"

"So, you mean..." Excitement buzzed through her, and she scissored her feet, squealing with joy. "You're staying?"

Sammi bit her lip, waiting as the bull looked at her

through his deep, espresso-colored eyes. Then he smiled, and his entire face blossomed. She could hardly breathe for the love and happiness she saw shining in his adoring gaze.

Just imagine, the *wedgie hedgie* herself had found and claimed a mate!

Joyful sniff.

"Of course, I am staying, Red. How could I ever leave you?"

"Oh, Sergio." She sighed and melted into him, snagging his lips in a long, languorous kiss despite all the FUCs, PRICs, and ASSs milling about.

"Let's get out of here," he growled against her lips, and she had to admit she loved that Jersey accent of his. Who else could make *heeya* sound so awesome?

That rumbly growl of his that started deep inside his chest and vibrated onto hers had her girly bits blushing and swelling with need. She wanted him so much. More now that she'd had a taste.

"You got me, Red. Every single inch."

"Good," she sighed, and she meant it.

She loved all his inches. Every last one. And there sure were a lot of them.

"Come on, Red." He stood up and led her to the car they'd borrowed from Director Cooper. "We'll let everyone else take point while you and I get to know each other."

"Oh, really?"

"Yes, really."

"I'll agree if you tell me one thing."

"What's that?"

"Why do you call me Red? You said it the very first time you saw me. But my hair is dark." She turned to face him and noted Sergio's cheeks were currently the only crimson things in the car.

"Well, you see..." he began then sucked in a breath.

He held it in for a moment before releasing it. *Like some form of meditation*, she thought. Then he turned to her with his heart in his eyes and damn if her own didn't swell three sizes right there.

"I call you Red, sweetheart, because to me you're like a red flag waving in front of my bull," he said.

"You mean I vex you?"

Sammi exhaled, a little disappointed. She was confused. Yes, they were mates, but not all mates loved each other. Still, her hedgie was anxious to hear him out.

"No! Well, maybe a little"—he chuckled—"but only when you go off and get yourself kidnapped."

"Oh, I see, so I am vexing, but you think it's okay?"

She sniffed, mildly placated.

"You are interesting, Red. You can't deny that. Vexing, too, but certainly not in any way I can't handle." He took her hand in his big, warm one and kissed her fingers.

"But what I mean is you are my red flag, waving just for me and my bull."

"Is that a good thing? What if I drive you nuts? What if the wedgie hedgie strikes again and I cause some major disaster?"

"Hell yeah it's a good thing," he growled.

"Sergio, be serious." She worried her lip.

"I am serious. Seriously crazy about you. I mean just looking at you drives me nuts, Red. Knowing you exist in this world with me is pure magic. You are 100 percent amazing," he crooned, and sucker that she was, her hedgie's heart melted. "A red flag isn't a bad thing at all, sweetheart. You're my weakness, my strength, my whole heart, this mystical force calling me, tempting me, pulling me toward you. I am dazzled by you, Red."

"You are?"

"Fuck yeah."

"Take me home. Show me," she demanded, and her bold bovine beamed at her in his happiness before pressing the pedal to the metal.

Twenty minutes later, the two of them were wrapped around each other with nothing between them at all. Sergio's magnificent cock pressed between her pussy lips, begging entrance, and she widened her legs, cradling his enormous girth as she welcomed him inside of her.

"Heaven, Red. Being inside you is pure heaven," he growled, crushing his mouth to hers.

Sammi had never had much luck with men, but kissing Sergio, making love to him, had her feeling like a goddess. He stretched her walls with his mighty thickness, impaling her over and over again with his forceful thrusts.

"Sergio," she moaned, and then she couldn't speak at all.

"Mate," he growled and pumped faster, harder, swirling his hips and touching her in the perfect spot so deep inside she thought she saw stars.

She didn't think she could take anymore, but he proved her wrong. Rising up onto his knees, he took her legs and pulled them up against his shoulders. Every slide of his cock drove her wild.

From this position, she felt every inch of his thickness get sucked down even deeper by her greedy pussy.

Hell yeah. He was gorgeous and insatiable. And holy hell, he was making her come. Sammi bit her lip, but her bull would have none of that. With blunt fingers, he tugged her flesh gently from her teeth.

"Lemme hear you, Red. I want that scream. It's mine," he growled, eyes glowing gold with his beast.

"Yes! Oh, Sergio!" She howled his name as her back

arched, wringing out every single inch of pleasure she could take from him.

"Red!" he screamed soon after.

His movements were rough, jerky, almost violent, but no less deep, no less tender. Sergio came hard, bathing her sheath with his cum, making her see stars.

They lay there a while without moving, a boneless heap of limbs struggling to breathe. Sammi had never felt so well-loved in all her life.

"It's 'cause I do, Red," her bull growled as he righted their positions and draped a cool sheet over their damp bodies.

"What?" she asked, not realizing she'd spoken aloud.

"I love you, Samantha Marie Andrews." He grinned and moved to kiss her.

Sammi was game, but she needed to set him straight about one thing. She pulled back at the last second, causing him to frown.

"Call me Red," she commanded.

"You sure?"

"Hell yeah. I'm Jersey sure about you, my big-hearted bovine."

Of course, she pronounced it *shawww*.

"Oh, you're gonna pay for that. Makin' fun of my accent," he growled.

Sammi giggled as Sergio found her tickle spots in no time at all. She was more than willing to pay the price for messing with her bull.

"I'm gonna like being mated," he said, kissing her lips when he finally gained the upper hand and settled over her.

She wasn't about to tell him she let him win. He could figure that out later.

EPILOGUE

"Pssssst! Harrison!"

"Yes, boss?"

"I think they're gone," Dr. Ranklinger whispered as he crawled through the sludge filling the septic tank beneath the abandoned *Critter Control* building he'd been using as a base of operations for months.

His hair-brained daughter, *no*, he wouldn't call her that, his *subject* had gotten them caught. Ugh. He knew she'd be trouble from the beginning, but what could he do? After her mother had died, relatives had sent her to him, and he had no choice but to try to cure the child of her shifter woes.

Unfortunately, he might have messed a few things up psychologically, but he was not going to admit that to anyone. For a while, she'd done well securing their funding through stolen identities that hurt no one important. Just shifters who he then sought to cure. They should be grateful, really.

"Yeah, but maste— I mean Dr. Ranklinger, I think your test subjects have been rounded up by FUC and PRIC."

"Never fear, Harrison. We shall get more test subjects. I

will rid the world of the shifter menace once and for all! My new formula is almost ready."

"Oh, how brave and noble you are! Treating us poor, lowly creatures! Bless you, master! Shifter Capture Alteration and Removal will be a great success! I just know it." Harrison trembled in his glee.

"Yes, I am noble and brave. Come on, it is time to retreat back to our *Place of Operations Proper*."

"Can I, master?"

"Oh fine, Harrison, go ahead," he relented.

"Back home to POOP!"

"Ugh." Dr. Ranklinger shook his head.

He might have to deal with cretins like Harrison for now, but soon the world would know of all he'd done to cure the shifter disease plaguing them. And he would get his daughter, *cough*, subject back too.

I AM EVER GONNA GET anything right? Julietta wondered as she walked across the FUCN'A courtyard to WANC. Seeing Tony, and Sofia had been great. So great she thought she'd stick around. But why did she have to run into *him* of all people?

Stupid stuck-up snobby snake-man!

Squeak! Even her mouse had something to say whenever she was around Dr. Damon Finn. The man was just so... so...

Gorgeous. Sexy. Hot.

Ugh. It was hopeless. She was a sucker for men who ignored her. And ignoring her was easy to do considering she was mousy, even for a mouse.

How was a girl like her going to get a guy like him to

notice she existed? Then it hit her as she passed the office of the registrar.

OMG. Brilliant!

Julietta knew exactly how to build her confidence and make an impact on the world.

She was going to get FUC'd!

The End

Or is it?

Damon Finn could not believe the little mouse shifter was his fated mate. Even worse, she'd gone awol! What else can this serpentine surgeon do, except follow her to FUCN'A? Find out what happens next in Mouse and the Ball by C.D. Gorri coming in 2022!

And there are more FUC Academy books from other authors coming your way soon!

To find out more about these books and more, visit worlds.EveLanglais.com or sign up for the EveL Worlds newsletter. If you haven't already downloaded the **free Academy intro** (written by Eve Langlais) make sure you grab it at worlds.evelanglais.com/wordpress/book/fucacademy1!

AN UNOFFICIAL GLOSSARY & ACRONYM APPENDIX

Zia- (zee-ah) aunt
Zio- (zee-oh) uncle
Oofa – (oo-fah) emphatic sigh
Nonna – (no-na) Grandmother
Impastata- (im-pahs-tata) mixed ricotta cheese
Bruthah- Brother in New Jerseyan
Heeyah- Here in New Jerseyan
Fuhgeddaboudit – how wise guys say forget about it
Shawww- Sure in New Jerseyan

FUC: Furry United Coalition
FUCN'A: Furry United Coalition Newbie Academy
WANC: Working and Administration Networking Core
ARSHOL: The Animal Rescue Special House of Learning
ASS: Avian Soaring Security
PRIC: Private Resourceful Investigative Contractors
DIC: Detective in Charge
COC: Complaints on Campus
HARD: Habitable Accords & Resolutions Document

HARDER COC: Habitable Accords & Resolution Document En Response to a Complaint on Campus form
MMM: Maude's Meatless Meals to go is Maude's food delivered (pronounced like mmmm)
HOLE: Home Office for Life-Threatening Emergencies (pop-up medical clinics used by multi-organizational task forces during operations)

ALSO BY C.D. GORRI

Someone has been stealing meatless meatballs from the FUCN'A cafeteria!

Conflict Resolution & Situation De-escalation Counselor Sofia Pelosi must discover the culprit before the vegetarian cadets' revolt, but she doesn't know where to begin.

Tony Leeds is a private investigator who specializes in locating missing shifters. He's tracked one to FUCN'A but is denied his request to search their records.

When word gets out there's a meatball bandit on campus, Tony offers to help the curly-haired woman who causes his inner Devil to think naughty thoughts. Will she scratch his back in return?

ABOUT THE AUTHOR

C.D. Gorri is an International Bestseller and Award-Winning author of steamy paranormal romance and urban fantasy. She is the creator of the Grazi Kelly Universe.

An avid reader with a profound love for books and literature, when she is not writing or taking care of her family, she can usually be found with a book or tablet in hand. C.D. lives in her home state of New Jersey where many of her characters or stories are based. Her tales are fast paced yet detailed with satisfying conclusions.

If you enjoy powerful heroines and loyal heroes who face relatable problems in supernatural settings, journey into the Grazi Kelly Universe. You will find sassy, curvy heroines and sexy, love-driven heroes who find their HEAs between the pages. Werewolves, Bears, Dragons, Tigers, Witches,

Romani, Lynxes, Foxes, Thunderbirds, Vampires, and many more Shifters and supernatural creatures dwell within her worlds. The most important thing is every mate in this universe is fated, loyal, and true lovers always get their happily-ever-afters.

C.D.'s website: cdgorri.com

CD's Newsletter sign-up: cdgorri.com/newsletter

C.D.'s Paranormal Pack Facebook reader group: facebook.-com/groups/CDGorrisParanormalPack

facebook.com/Cdgorribooks
twitter.com/cgor22
instagram.com/cdgorri
goodreads.com/cdgorri
bookbub.com/authors/c-d-gorri

www.ingramcontent.com/pod-product-compliance
Ingram Content Group UK Ltd.
Pitfield, Milton Keynes, MK11 3LW, UK
UKHW040007200726
13854UKWH00001B/77

9 798201 029968

THE ALCHEMY OF RESILIENT LEADERSHIP

HOW CAN YOU LEAD AND SUCCEED DESPITE CHANGE AND CHALLENGES?

DR. AMIT DAS

Made with ♥ on the Notion Press Platform
www.notionpress.com